Steven sank down on the edge of his bed and stared into space. He wasn't sure what time it was, and he didn't care. He just knew he was happier than he had been in a long, long time.

With a sigh, he took his wallet out. Sliding his fingers into a hidden pocket behind his ID card and license, he pulled out a worn photograph. Tricia's face smiled back at him.

"I can't believe I found you again," he whispered.

Then his gaze fell on the wall over his desk. A photograph of Cara and him at the state fair drew his attention. Steven's stomach sank.

He truly loved Cara. But seeing Andrea that night had stirred up feelings he hadn't realized he still had. And he knew that, as much as he loved Cara, he desperately wanted to see Andrea again.

Bantam Books in the Sweet Valley High Series
Ask your bookseller for the books you have missed

SWEET VALLEY HIGH

THE GHOST OF TRICIA MARTIN

Written by
Kate William

Created by
FRANCINE PASCAL

BANTAM BOOKS
NEW YORK · TORONTO · LONDON · SYDNEY · AUCKLAND

RL 6, IL age 12 and up

THE GHOST OF TRICIA MARTIN
A Bantam Book / April 1990

Sweet Valley High is a registered trademark of Francine Pascal

Conceived by Francine Pascal

Produced by Daniel Weiss Associates, Inc.
33 West 17th Street
New York, NY 10011

Cover art by James Mathewuse

ISBN 0-553-28487-8

Published simultaneously in the United States and Canada

Bantam Books are published by Bantam Books, a division of Bantam Doubleday
Dell Publishing Group, Inc. Its trademark, consisting of the words "Bantam
Books" and the portrayal of a rooster, is Registered in U.S. Patent and Trademark
Office and in other countries. Marca Registrada. Bantam Books, 666 Fifth Avenue,
New York, New York 10103.

PRINTED IN THE UNITED STATES OF AMERICA

OPM   0 9 8 7 6 5 4 3 2 1

One

"Jessica," Elizabeth Wakefield muttered under her breath as she hunted through her makeup drawer in the bathroom for her new eyeliner. When she couldn't find it, she slammed the drawer closed and opened her twin sister's drawer on the other side of the sink. There, in plain view, was the eyeliner. Elizabeth shook her head as she uncapped it.

"Oops, I forgot to tell you I borrowed that," Jessica apologized, strolling into the bathroom from her bedroom. She perched on the counter next to Elizabeth. "Going out with Todd tonight?"

"How did you ever guess?" Elizabeth looked in the mirror and grinned.

"I guess it's just my natural brilliance, Liz," Jessica said.

The two sisters caught each other's eye in the mirror. Together, they made a perfect pair of California girls. Both had wavy, honey-blond hair and eyes the color of the Pacific Ocean. They had the same heart-shaped faces and size-six figures, the same musical voices and bubbly laughs. Right down to the dimples in their left cheeks, Elizabeth and Jessica Wakefield were identical.

But that was only on the surface, as any one of their friends in Sweet Valley High's junior class would immediately point out. Elizabeth, who was older than Jessica by four minutes, was thoughtful and responsible. She could lose herself for hours in a book, and she gave her heart and soul to the three most important people in her life: her boyfriend, Todd Wilkins, her best friend, Enid Rollins, and her twin sister, Jessica. Whenever something was troubling her, she was likely to work it out for herself by writing about it in her journal. Elizabeth was not the sort of person to publicize her private thoughts.

But there was never any doubt about how "Hurricane Jessica" felt. She went from one extreme to the other, from boyfriend to boyfriend, and from one fad to the next. She loved nothing more than being the center of attention and wasn't above cooking up a scheme to make sure she stayed there. "As subtle as a blow torch," Elizabeth lovingly described her, and Jessica never argued. So, as identical as the twins seemed at first glance, they were really quite different.

"That's a good color," Jessica said as Elizabeth smudged the eyeliner carefully at the corners of her eyes. "It's very sophisticated."

"Yeah, I noticed how much you like it," Elizabeth teased. She glanced at her twin and grinned. "So, where are *you* going tonight?"

Jessica slid off the counter, her face instantly clouded by irritation. "That beach party, and I have to get a ride from Lila. It makes me *soooo* mad. Why does the Fiat have to break down *now*?"

The twins shared a Fiat Spider convertible they had inherited from their mother. At least, they shared it when it worked. Two days before, when Jessica had been ready to leave cheerleading practice, it had simply refused to start. The mechanic still wasn't sure if the problem was as simple as a worn fan belt or as serious as

3

a blown transmission. So for the past two days the twins had had to find rides from their friends.

"What's wrong with getting a ride from Lila?" Elizabeth asked. She recapped the pencil and put it in her drawer. "She's your best friend."

Jessica gave her an exaggerated look of disgust. "Oh, come on, Liz, that's not the point. I like to be able to leave when I want. I can't stand having to wait for someone to pick me up."

Elizabeth shrugged. It didn't seem like such a big deal to her, but that was Jessica, blowing things out of proportion as usual.

"Why don't you borrow Mom's car?" Elizabeth suggested.

Jessica closed her eyes. "Go to the beach party in a *station wagon*? Forget it." She shuddered dramatically.

"Well, all I can say is, you have my deepest sympathy."

There was a knock on the door of Elizabeth's bedroom, which adjoined the bathroom. "Liz?" came a voice.

"Just a minute, Steve," Elizabeth called. She crossed her room and opened the door for her brother. Jessica followed her.

Steven was home from college for a few weeks,

working on an independent study project. At the moment, however, he didn't look like he had his mind on his books. His dark hair was still wet from the shower, and he was wearing khaki pants with a knife-edge crease. In his hands were two brand-new shirts. As he walked into the room, he held up the shirts.

"Which of these do you think I should wear tonight?" he asked the twins. "The blue one or the green one?"

Jessica poked her brother in the ribs and headed for the door. "Lucky Cara," she teased. "I hope she's getting dressed up, too, if you're going to look so sharp." She waved and went into her bedroom, closing the door.

Elizabeth had been watching Steven intently while Jessica spoke, and she had seen a blush color his cheeks.

"You're not going out with Cara tonight, are you?" Elizabeth said in a low voice.

Steven shook his head. Cara Walker, who was one of Jessica's close friends, was Steven's girlfriend. It was a warm, caring relationship, but Elizabeth knew something had happened recently to turn it upside down. Her brother had seen a ghost.

Not in the real sense, of course. But the way

5

it had shaken Steven, Elizabeth decided it could just as well have been a ghost. The day before, Steven had gone with Elizabeth to the Sweet Valley Mall, and they had stopped in a store called the Unique Boutique. Standing behind the counter had been a girl who looked, sounded, and dressed just like Tricia Martin, the girlfriend Steven had lost to leukemia months ago. Elizabeth knew she would never forget the look of astonishment and wonder that had crossed her brother's face when he saw her. He had been unable to resist asking the girl's name, and his eyes had devoured her. Elizabeth had been frightened by his intensity.

"Are you going out with *her?*" Elizabeth asked Steven. "With Andrea?"

"Well, actually . . ." Steven looked at her steadily. "Yes, I am seeing Andrea tonight." His gaze wavered, and he looked down.

Elizabeth tried to make her voice sound light. "Do you really think that's a great idea?" she asked. "I mean, why bring back all those sad memories?"

Steven shrugged in a feeble attempt at nonchalance. "I know it sounds crazy, but I just have to go out with her once. You know, to prove to myself she isn't really like Tricia at all."

6

"Just because she looks a bit like Tricia doesn't mean she's anything like her," Elizabeth said.

Nodding, Steven said, "I know! That's my whole point. So it's just this once—I probably won't even like her at all, once we start talking." He looked down at the shirts he was holding and laughed. "She probably likes everything I *don't* like and vice versa."

Elizabeth had a feeling Steven was more interested in Andrea than he was letting on, and that worried her. Tricia was gone forever. If Steven thought he had found a way to bring her back, he might be letting himself in for heartache all over again—not to mention what it would do to Cara.

"Just don't forget about Cara," Elizabeth warned gently. "You could end up hurting her a lot."

"Hurting her?" Steven protested. "Come on, I would never hurt Cara. But I just have to get this out of my system, Liz. Then I can go on."

Elizabeth didn't say anything; she just looked at her brother with concern.

"Listen—promise you won't tell anyone, OK?" Steven asked in a tight voice. "It's not that there's anything to hide, but there's just no

7

point in letting Cara find out. She wouldn't understand."

"I think she would," Elizabeth said. "If you really mean it when you say you only want to see Andrea once, I think Cara would understand. She knows how much you loved Tricia."

Steven shook his head and turned away. "Liz, just—I don't want—"

There was a sudden blast of music as Jessica turned on the stereo in her room. Steven cast a look in that direction and then turned to Elizabeth again.

"Especially Jess," he said in a low voice. "You know she can never keep a secret. If Cara hears about this, she might get the wrong idea."

Elizabeth frowned. "If you're worried about Cara finding out, why don't you tell her yourself?"

"Liz, just promise, please?" Steven asked.

Reluctantly, Elizabeth nodded. "All right. I won't say anything about it."

Steven stepped forward and gave her a quick, hard hug. "You're the best, Liz. Thanks." He turned and hurried down the hall to his own room. Elizabeth closed her bedroom door and walked over to her bureau. She picked up a brush and absently began brushing her hair. *I just hope he knows what he's doing,* she thought.

With one last critical look at herself, she went downstairs to wait for Todd. She was about to go into her father's study to say goodbye to her parents when angry voices stopped her. She stood still, her hand on the doorknob.

"I'm sorry, Ned! But I don't know what you think I can do about it!" Alice Wakefield said.

"Maybe if you had called the electrician last month instead of waiting until the problem got worse, it wouldn't have cost twice as much as it should have!" Mr. Wakefield returned. "Now they're charging us two hundred dollars for what should have been a simple job!"

Elizabeth bit her lower lip. She hated to hear her parents argue. It always made her feel so helpless. She knew it was perfectly normal for people to have disagreements, but it used to be rare for her parents to argue. Lately, it had been happening a little more often.

"You're the one who said it wasn't a serious problem, Ned, so don't blame *me*."

Elizabeth could hear that her mother was walking toward the door, and she knew she had to do something quickly. She turned the handle and pushed open the door, nearly hitting her mother. Both parents stared at her, startled. There was a moment of embarrassed silence.

"Todd's picking me up in a few minutes," Elizabeth said at last, glancing from her mother to her father. "I just wanted to say good night."

Alice Wakefield brushed her blond hair back with one hand. Then she sent Elizabeth a warm smile. "OK, honey. Have a good time."

"I will, Mom," Elizabeth said. She searched her mother's face anxiously, but the tension seemed to be gone. Elizabeth smiled at her father. "Good night, Dad."

" 'Night, sweetie," Mr. Wakefield replied. He shuffled some papers together on his desk and winked at her. "Don't stay out too late, hold up a bank, or anything like that."

Elizabeth had to laugh at his silliness. "I won't. I promise." She crossed the room and gave him a light kiss on his cheek. Then she hurried out of the den.

Two

Steven wiped his forehead with the back of his hand. His mind was racing with a million different things to say to Andrea.

Out of habit, he clicked his high beams off as a car approached. He stared ahead at the road, remembering Tricia's last days. She had been so pale and distant, just like a dream that had faded before his eyes. Steven would never forget the terrible anguish of losing her, of loving her with all his heart and knowing that that wasn't enough to save her.

He took a deep breath and tried to stay calm. Up ahead, waiting for him in an intimate Pacific Shores restaurant, was Andrea. It was more than he could have wished for, to have a second chance. Steven's heart raced with exhilaration and hope.

When he reached the restaurant in Pacific Shores, he was so nervous that his hands were shaking. He parked his car, got out, and, after taking another deep breath, he headed toward the restaurant.

He saw her the moment he walked in, and his heart leapt inside his chest. For the space of several heartbeats he stood still, just staring at her. Then he hurried over to the table.

"Hi," Steven gasped, drinking in each detail of her face. "Sorry I'm late."

"No, I was a little early," she said. She smiled back and swept a curl off her forehead.

For a moment, Steven didn't know what to say. She was so much like Tricia in her voice and her gestures. Even the pretty green blouse with a lace collar she was wearing was similar to one Tricia had owned.

Andrea arched her eyebrows. "Are you all right?"

"Sure! I'm fine!" Steven said, sitting down. There was a moment of awkward silence, and then Steven mumbled, "You look nice."

"Thanks." Andrea smiled warmly.

They shared a long look, and Steven felt a wave of emotion that threatened to carry him off.

"Listen," Steven said, leaning forward earnestly. "Do you like walking on the beach?"

"Mmm!" Andrea was sipping her water, and she nodded. "Sure. Doesn't everyone?"

"I knew you would," he said. "I feel like I already know you so well."

"How could you?" Andrea asked, laughing and shaking her head. "We just met."

Steven smiled. "It doesn't seem that way to me."

A delicate blush tinged her cheeks. "That's so sweet," she murmured.

All the warnings Steven had given himself disappeared. He could not stop marveling at how lucky he was to have found her! It was a dream come true.

He wanted to touch her, but he didn't dare. "Tricia, I have a feeling we're going to have a great time tonight."

Just then the waiter appeared, and the next few minutes were taken up by ordering dinner. "The chef's salad is really great," Steven suggested. It had been Tricia's favorite.

13

"That sounds good," Andrea said without enthusiasm.

After they ordered, the conversation turned to Steven's independent study project. Andrea listened intently, her expression thoughtful. She had the same reflective, quiet way of listening, Steven thought, that he had loved so much in Tricia.

Steven hardly tasted his food when it came because he was so caught up in talking to Andrea. But she finally interrupted him.

"Steve, no offense," she began quietly, "but you've called me Tricia three times."

"Steven looked both startled and embarrassed. "I-I'm sorry," he stammered. "I didn't realize— it's just that—"

"Just what?" she prompted in a gentle voice.

"You remind me of her so—" Steven's throat closed up suddenly, and tears came to his eyes. He tried to cover up by coughing harshly, but he had to wipe his eyes.

Andrea leaned toward him and put her hand on his. "Who was she?" she asked. Her voice was low and earnest, and her eyes were warmly sympathetic.

Haltingly, Steven began to tell Andrea about

14

Tricia. He described her last days and the love he had had for her. At first he had thought he wouldn't be able to speak about it, but Andrea's sincerity gave him the strength.

"I don't understand how life can be so unfair," he concluded bitterly. He shook his head, his heart aching. "Someone as good and wonderful as she was. She never hurt anyone in her life."

Andrea had tears in her eyes. "I'm so sorry," she whispered. "That's so sad. I felt the same way when my grandfather died in a car crash. I thought, why did it have to be him?"

"I knew you'd understand," Steven said in a husky voice. He took a deep breath.

"I guess you must miss her a lot," Andrea ventured.

Steven frowned. "Well, that's the thing," he said. He looked at her wonderingly. "When I saw you—" He saw the puzzled look on her face and tried to explain. "You look just like her—and sound and act like her, too," he said in a rush.

Andrea's puzzlement turned to surprise. "Oh. Is that why you asked me out?"

"No! I mean—" Steven felt terrible. "I knew I would like you," he stammered. "And I do."

She smiled. "I like you, too," she said in a quiet voice.

Steven exhaled heavily. "That's great," he breathed, smiling at her. "That's great."

There was a long silence. Steven wanted to jump out of his chair and start yelling with happiness, but he refrained.

Finally, Andrea said, "Thanks for dinner."

"Thanks for accepting," Steven answered. He smiled. "Can I call you again?"

Andrea tipped her head to one side, a playful grin on her face. "I guess so."

"Great." Steven laughed. "I think I'll call you when I get home tonight."

Andrea let out a laugh, too. "Why don't you wait until tomorrow to call?" she suggested.

"OK, if I have to." Steven couldn't stop smiling. He was on top of the world.

Jessica hopped out of Lila's car at the beach parking lot and breathed in deeply. "Mmm . . . smell that?" she asked her friend.

"What?" Lila replied. "The ocean?"

Jessica grinned impishly. "No—available guys."

"I know what you mean," Lila agreed with a giggle. "Let's go!"

Together, they trudged through the deep sand toward a big group of kids. Music filled the air, and whoops of excitement drifted over from around the volleyball net. Jessica felt a familiar tingle of anticipation. Going to parties was high on her list of favorite things to do.

"Do you see your friend from Palisades?" she asked Lila.

Lila was scanning the crowd. There were a few Sweet Valley students, but mostly the people were from the Big Mesa and Palisades high schools. A friend of Lila's from Palisades had invited them.

"There she is," Lila said, pointing to a group of girls sitting in a circle. They all seemed to be focused on one person still hidden from view.

Jessica surveyed the group as she took a step nearer. Then she saw that the girls were listening to a boy playing a guitar. From a distance, she couldn't tell why he had drawn such a large crowd. He wasn't especially good-looking. In fact, he had a serious, angry look on his face. But all of the girls around him were mesmerized.

"Come on," Lila said, leading the way. "Hi, Angie," she called out.

One of the girls sitting across from the guitar player, a cute, diminutive blonde with bouncy curls, looked up and waved. Without speaking, she beckoned them closer.

Intrigued, Jessica followed Lila to the circle and sat down in the sand by Angie. *There has to be more to that boy than meets the eye*, she thought.

"Hi, Angie, this is Jessica," Lila said with a casual wave of one hand.

Angie smiled. "Hi," she whispered.

Jessica glanced at the boy, who was singing in a low voice. "Who's he?" she asked quietly.

"Keith," Angie breathed in an admiring voice. "He's so deep."

"Really?" Jessica looked over at him again with a speculative gleam in her eyes. On closer inspection, she decided that there was something attractive about him. His thick brown hair fell across his forehead as he bent over the guitar. He was wearing a "No Nukes" T-shirt and old jeans, and his feet were bare. *Not very stylish*, Jessica thought, but she could see he had an athletic build under his sloppy clothes.

"What makes him so—um, deep?" Lila asked, trickling sand through her fingers.

Angie bit her lip and gazed up at the sky for a moment. "Mmm. Well, he's really into ecology and world peace. Stuff like that."

"A do-gooder," Lila decided in a bored tone. One of the girls nearby heard her and sent Lila an indignant frown. Lila gave her a haughty look.

Jessica didn't say anything, but she watched Keith steadily. She felt a playful urge to test her charms. It would be fun to see if she could flirt successfully with such a serious, no-nonsense boy. She kept her eyes on him, waiting for her chance.

At last, Keith finished his song and glanced up. When his gaze rested on her, Jessica gave him a brilliant smile. Spontaneously, Keith smiled back. Jessica didn't waste a moment; she stood up and crossed the circle to sit next to him. Most of the other girls stood up and drifted toward the bigger crowd.

"Hi," Jessica said. "What was that song you were just singing? I couldn't hear all the words."

Keith pushed his hair off his forehead. "It's about the industrial giants devouring the land," he said with a challenging note in his voice. "You probably wouldn't have liked it."

But Jessica nodded seriously. "I bet I would, if I could hear it again," she told him.

"For real?" Keith turned to her with a reappraising look.

"For real," Jessica replied. "It's not the kind of thing you hear on the radio. That stuff is so—superficial," she finished.

Nodding, Keith said, "I know what you mean. Most of it is just noise pollution."

"Sing it again, OK?" Jessica urged, moving closer. She gave him another melting smile. "Please?"

Keith grinned. Without the angry scowl, he looked positively cute. The party was turning out to be a lot better than she had anticipated!

At home, Steven sank down on the edge of his bed and stared into space. He wasn't sure what time it was, and he didn't care. He just knew he was happier than he had been in a long, long time.

With a sigh, he took out his wallet. Sliding his fingers into a hidden pocket behind his ID card and license, he pulled out a worn photograph. Tricia's face smiled back at him.

"I can't believe I found you again," he whispered.

Then his gaze fell on the wall over his desk. A photograph of Cara and him at the state fair drew his attention. Steven's stomach sank.

"What am I doing?" he asked himself. He shoved Tricia's photograph back in his wallet and stood up. He truly loved Cara. But seeing Andrea that night had stirred up feelings he hadn't realized he still had. And he knew that, as much as he loved Cara, he desperately wanted to see Andrea again.

Three

Elizabeth sat at her desk on Saturday morning, chewing on the end of her pen. In front of her were several crossed-out paragraphs for an article she was writing for the school newspaper, *The Oracle*. She had been working on the article for an hour, and she wasn't pleased with one sentence she had written. Feeling frustrated, Elizabeth tossed her pen onto the desk and sat back.

"Liz?" There was a tap at the door, and then Steven opened it and put his head in. "Hi. Am I bothering you?"

Elizabeth's face lit up. "Hey, Steve. No, I'm giving up on this. What's new?"

"Oh, not much," he said casually. Steven sat on the edge of Elizabeth's bed. His eyes were glowing with excitement.

"Not much?" Elizabeth tipped her head to one side. "Come on, tell me."

Her brother let his breath out slowly and squared his shoulders. "Liz—last night—it was amazing. Andrea's so much like Tricia, it's just incredible!"

"Really?" Elizabeth gave him a faint smile. "I know she looks like Tricia, but—"

"No! That's just it!" Steven cut in. "She's *exactly* like Tricia, in every way! She likes all the same things Tricia did, and she dresses like her. She talks like her! Everything! It was like being in a time warp!"

The expression in Steven's eyes made Elizabeth uneasy. Frowning, she looked down at her hands. Nobody was *just* like anybody else, not even identical twins. She knew that better than anyone.

"We met at La Paloma, where Tricia and I used to go all the time," Steven went on eagerly. "She looked so *right* there! And when I told her how good the chef's salad was, she ordered that, just like Tricia!"

Steven jumped up and began pacing. He

couldn't seem to contain his enthusiasm. He kept picking things up and putting them down. Elizabeth watched him silently.

"And she told me how much she likes to walk on the beach, just like Tricia used to. I still can't get over it."

"Steve—" Elizabeth chose her words carefully. "Steve, she's not Tricia, remember. She's a different person who just happens to be like her in some ways."

Steven waved his hand irritably. "Look, I know she's a different person—I'm not crazy."

"I didn't say that," Elizabeth put in.

"I know, but. . . ." Steven abruptly stopped pacing. He sank onto the bed and ran his hands through his hair. "Maybe I *am* acting a little crazy. But I just can't get her out of my mind. I have to see her again."

Elizabeth gave him a hard look. "Are you going to break up with Cara?"

"No! Of course not, it's not like that!" Steven stared at the floor for a long moment. Then he shook his head.

"It's not like what?" Elizabeth asked.

Steven sighed. "I don't know, maybe you're right. I should try to stop thinking about her. I don't want to break up with Cara, because I really do love her a lot. Maybe I should find some way to keep my mind off this whole thing."

"I think so," Elizabeth agreed.

Agitated, Steven stood up and began pacing again. He stopped at Elizabeth's bureau and picked up a sports magazine that was lying there. On the cover was a breathtaking photograph of a man hang gliding. Steven riffled the pages and grinned. "From your 'Fearless Elizabeth' campaign?"

"Right." Elizabeth chuckled.

Not long ago, Elizabeth had decided that she was too dull and predictable. Everyone took it for granted that Jessica did wild and exciting things and that Elizabeth was steady as a rock. So she had tried to shake up her life a little by perming her hair, taking surfing lessons, and doing exactly what everyone expected her *not* to do. She had even toyed with the idea of hang gliding but had decided against it. For one thing it was dangerous, and for another, it was just too expensive.

Steven had researched hang gliding, however, and given it a lot of thought. "Maybe I should take hang-gliding lessons," he said. "If I concentrate on them, I won't be thinking about Tricia—I mean, Andrea."

"If you really want to get your mind off Andrea, why don't you spend more time with Cara?" Elizabeth suggested.

Her brother looked at her guiltily, but didn't say anything. Elizabeth was trying to stay sympathetic and see things from his point of view. But it looked to her as though Steven was letting his memories of the past take over the present.

"I think I *will* take lessons," Steven decided, putting down the magazine. "I can pay for them with the money I earned last summer."

Elizabeth sighed and turned away. "I doubt hang guiding will solve your problems, Steve," she said.

"Look, Liz," Steven said angrily. "I loved Tricia more than anyone! You're not being fair!"

"Are you being fair?" she replied. "Are you being fair to Cara or Andrea?"

Steven stared at her for a tense moment. Then he stalked out of the room. Elizabeth leaned forward and rested her forehead on her hands.

"Don't do it, Steve," she whispered. "This is a terrible idea."

Sitting back, she scowled at her botched article for a few seconds, then crumpled it up and went downstairs for breakfast.

*   *   *

Jessica sliced open another orange for the juicer. "I met this gorgeous guy at the beach party last night," she announced to her family.

"That's nice," Mrs. Wakefield replied, continuing to read the newspaper.

"You meet gorgeous guys every day," Elizabeth added. She sounded grumpy.

Jessica shrugged. "Not like this guy," she said airily. "It's not just that he's so gorgeous. He's totally *dedicated*."

Mr. Wakefield let out a short laugh and flipped open the sports section. "That's fast work, Jessica."

"Not to *me*," Jessica declared. She gave her father a sharp look and poured out some fresh orange juice. "He's dedicated to the world. The whole world. He has all these great ideals. He's so interesting."

When nobody pounced on her lead, Jessica let out a disgusted sigh. Sometimes her family was a big disappointment to her. Instead of wanting to know all about Keith, they just buried themselves in the paper and ignored her. In fact, everyone at the table seemed to be in a sour mood except her.

Frowning, she slumped into her chair next to

28

Elizabeth and stared hard at her twin. Finally, Elizabeth looked up at the ceiling.

Elizabeth sighed. "OK, Jess. I want to know all the details. What's his name? What's he like?"

Jessica smiled happily. "His name is Keith," she gushed. "He's very serious, and he's interested in all these important world causes. Endangered species, alternative energy sources, greenhouses, stuff like that."

"Do you mean the greenhouse effect?" Elizabeth asked with the hint of a smile on her face.

Jessica snapped her fingers. "Right, that's it. I knew it was something like that."

"Jessica—our specialist in current events." Her father chuckled.

"Don't tell me," Mrs. Wakefield teased. "You're about to become an expert on the environment."

Jessica's eyes sparkled. "Well, who knows? If I spend some time with Keith, it might just rub off."

"An interesting choice of words," Elizabeth mumbled. Jessica giggled.

"So, what else does this wonder boy do?" Mr. Wakefield asked. "Is he in high school, or is he too busy saving the world for that?"

"Oh, Dad," Jessica said. "He goes to Palisades High."

"I thought you were through with do-gooders after Sheffield," Elizabeth said.

Jessica gasped. "That was *totally* different, Liz. Sheffield was such a bore about homeless people. A rich, cute bore, though," she added thoughtfully. For a little while, Sheffield Eastman had seemed like the boy of her dreams. Now he was ancient history.

Elizabeth grinned at her. "So? Did he ask you out? He wasn't too idealistic to notice you, was he?"

Everyone laughed, and Jessica gave them a smirk. If her whole family enjoyed giving her a hard time just because she liked to go out with a lot of boys, that was their problem.

"He isn't *that* idealistic," she replied confidently. "He asked me to help him hand out leaflets about recycling today. He doesn't have a car, though, because he doesn't believe in using fossil fuels or ruining the land with paved roads. So, Mom, can I borrow yours?"

Mr. Wakefield laughed. "He should move to China, where everyone travels by bicycle."

"Yuck." Jessica shuddered. "Mom? Can I?"

"Sorry, honey," her mother replied. She put down her coffee cup. "I'm taking a new client to the furniture showrooms all day today."

"What?" Mr. Wakefield sounded astonished. He was staring at his wife, and his smile had vanished. "We were supposed to drive up to White Canyon today for lunch."

The sudden silence around the breakfast table was electric. Jessica glanced from her mother to her father and back again. Alice Wakefield's career as a decorator kept her very busy, and Ned Wakefield's law practice often made him tense. Lately, they had been bickering more and more. Jessica knew they had arranged to spend the day together to get away from the pressure.

Jessica looked anxiously at her twin sister, who returned the look. Steven picked up a section of the paper and began to read. Jessica wished someone would say something to break the tension.

Mrs. Wakefield closed her eyes for a moment. "I'm so sorry, Ned. I forgot."

"How could you forget a thing like that? We've been planning this for two weeks! Am I so insignificant that our plans don't carry any weight at all?"

"Oh, Ned, don't take it so personally!" Alice Wakefield retorted. "I just *forgot*. This new client is very fussy, and when she said she had to go

31

to the furniture showrooms, I said I would take her. That's all." She picked up her coffee cup again, and Jessica saw her hand tremble slightly.

"Mom?" Elizabeth put in. "Do you think you could reschedule?"

Mrs. Wakefield took a sip of coffee before answering. She shook her head and managed a weak smile for Elizabeth. "No, that's a good idea, but Mrs. Petty insisted on doing it today."

"Great. That's just great." Mr. Wakefied said. He pushed his chair back and stood up. "If you're standing me up, I might as well go to the office myself." He strode out of the room.

Jessica gulped. It seemed that virtually every conversation between her parents was ending up this way lately.

A door slammed, and they all heard the motor of Mr. Wakefield's car race.

"Mom?" Elizabeth began, after a heavy pause.

Alice Wakefield stood up abruptly. "I'm going to be late, kids. I have to go."

Without looking at any of them, she grabbed her purse and hurried out the back door.

Four

Steven took his coffee into the den. He didn't want to think about why his parents were arguing so much. He had enough to think about as it was.

He glanced at the telephone on his father's desk. Frowning, he picked it up and dialed Andrea's number. At the first ring, however, he hung up. His hand hovered over the receiver while he stared at it. He knew he had to get her out of his mind, but it was harder than he wanted to admit.

After a moment, he picked it up again and dialed another number.

"Hello?" Cara answered.

"Hi, it's me," Steven said, relaxing back against the chair.

"Steve!" Her voice was bright. "I was just this second going to call you! We must have ESP."

Steven laughed. "I guess so," he said. "What do you want to do today?"

"Mmm . . . I don't know. What do you want to do?"

An image of Andrea floated into Steven's mind, and he closed his eyes tightly. He forced himself to think of Cara. All he needed to do was put a big dose of romance into their relationship, he figured. Then he would forget about Andrea. He rubbed his eyes and tried to concentrate.

"How about if I surprise you?" he said mysteriously.

Cara giggled. "Oh! No fair! Give me a hint, anyway. Just a teeny one."

Did Cara always sound so girly, so silly? Steven wondered. He immediately told himself she was merely bubbly, which was a good quality. Just hearing the trust and affection in her voice made him feel mean-spirited for mentally criticizing her.

I can't be dishonest with Cara, he told himself. *I'm not going to see Andrea again.*

"No hints," he told her. "That's what surprises are for. Besides, I don't even know what it's going to be yet."

"Boy, are you tough," Cara replied. "All right. What time will you pick me up?"

Steven glanced at his watch. "An hour?"

"OK. Bye."

After he hung up, Steven sat brooding for a few minutes. When he tried to think of something to do, he kept coming up with busy, strenuous activities that required a lot of concentration and energy. It wasn't that he was trying to run away from his problems, he told himself. He just needed to get out for a while. Hiking to Castle Rock up at Secca Lake would be perfect: it was a long hike, and a romantic spot. It was just what he needed to take his mind off Andrea.

An hour later, he stopped outside the apartment house where Cara lived with her mother. Cara waved from her window and after a few minutes came out the building door. She scrambled into the car next to him and kissed him on the cheek.

"Hi," she said. Her brown eyes were warm.

Steven looked at her for a long moment. She was very pretty, and so easygoing. He didn't want to hurt her in any way. Feeling like he had just made a New Year's resolution, he leaned over and gave her a warm, appreciative kiss.

"Hi," he said.

"*Hel*-lo," she said. She sat back and grinned. "So? Where are we going?"

Steven started the car and pulled away from the curb. "I thought we could go up to Secca Lake and take a hike to Castle Rock," he said.

"A hike?" Cara made a skeptical face and looked down at her feet. She was wearing white sandals with thin ankle straps.

Steven followed her gaze. "Oh, no. Do you want to go back?"

"No, that's OK." Cara laughed. She shook her head, and her brown ponytail bounced. "I don't mind."

"We don't have to hike if you don't want to," he insisted.

"I want to," Cara assured him. "Don't worry about it."

"If you say so." Steven shrugged.

"You would not believe what happened at cheerleading practice on Thursday," Cara said, sighing dramatically. She leaned back and laughed.

36

"Robin Wilson was doing this funny imitation of Chrome Dome Cooper. And we were all cracking up, but right in the middle of it, Mr. Cooper walks into the gym—"

Steven smiled weakly. "Yeah, Jessica already told me about it."

"Oh." Cara looked a little bit disappointed. "Well, forget it, then, if you already heard it."

Steven thought there was a touch of irritation in her voice. "Listen, I didn't mean it like that," he said quickly.

"No, forget it," Cara said.

He let his breath out slowly. Sometimes he wondered if Cara was a little too immature for him. It seemed she was always talking about cheerleading or shopping or going to parties.

But as soon as he thought that, he scolded himself for being so petty. She *wasn't* empty and childish, just enthusiastic and cheerful.

"So, I've gotten a lot of research done for my independent study project on legal ethics," Steven said to break the silence. "But I still have to interview some more people. I have appointments with two judges my dad knows, and I'll probably be able to start the paper next week."

Cara was busy examining her nails. "Oh, really?'' she asked while she frowned at her cuticles. ''That's great.''

Faintly irritated, Steven rested his elbow in the open window. They drove the rest of the way to Secca Lake in silence.

''We don't have to do this if you don't want to,'' Steven told Cara when they reached the beginning of the hiking trail. The weather was hot and steamy, and the sun glared behind a bright white haze.

Cara knelt down and adjusted the straps of her sandals. ''No, I'll be fine,'' she said.

''OK,'' Steven said. ''Let's go.''

After fifteen minutes, he began to wonder why he had thought a hike would be romantic. He was hot and sweaty, and he kept having to wait for Cara to catch up. When she stopped for the third time to adjust her sandals, he had to struggle to keep his patience.

''Uh-oh—I think I'm getting a blister,'' Cara said in a worried tone the next time she caught up. She took off one sandal and touched her bare heel with her thumb.

''Do you want to go back?'' Steven asked, controlling his voice carefully. He looked off into the distance. There was nothing romantic about the hike at all. And it wasn't getting his mind off anything.

Steven couldn't stop thinking about Andrea. Everything Cara did led him to a comparison of the two girls. Andrea would have been ready for anything, he was sure. She wouldn't have needed to rest, and certainly wouldn't have whined and complained. He felt certain that Andrea was mature and self-reliant.

Cara trustingly held out one hand so he could steady her while she put her sandal back on. When Steven touched her, he felt guilty again. As soon as he could, he took his hand away and shoved it in his back pocket. He had to think of something besides Andrea.

"I was thinking about learning hang gliding," he said abruptly. "What do you think about it?"

Cara grimaced. *"Hang gliding?"* she echoed in a skeptical voice. "Why would you want to do that? It seems so dangerous."

Steven felt resentment swell up in his chest. "I think it would be fun," he said stubbornly. "Are you saying I'm irresponsible?"

"I never said that!" Cara said. She looked surprised. "All I said was, it looks dangerous. Don't people always crash in those things?"

Steven clenched his jaw. "Not *always*. You

know, you could have said, 'Go for it, Steve, it must be great to fly.' "

That was what Andrea would have said, he thought. She would have seen how wonderful it could be to soar up in the clouds on hot air currents. But all Cara could do was throw cold water on his idea. She was trying to drag him down.

"I'm definitely doing it," he went on. "Every Sunday there's an orientation session. Tomorrow, I'm going to see about renting the equipment and taking lessons."

"OK. Fine," Cara replied shakily. "You asked me what I thought and I told you."

Steven turned away. "Fine. Ready to go?"

"I—" Cara didn't finish her sentence. She just bowed her head and followed Steven silently.

"I don't know why I'm doing this for you," Lila grumbled.

Jessica slid into the passenger seat and gave Lila a grateful smile. "Because you're such a wonderful, special, fantastic person, that's why."

"Yeah, right," Lila said, rolling her eyes.

After a long argument over the telephone, Jessica had finally convinced Lila to let her borrow Lila's car. Now Jessica had to ride back to Lila's house to drop her friend off. Once she was mobile, she could meet up with Keith.

"I'll see you later," Jessica said a few minutes later as she got into the driver's seat at Lila's house.

Lila walked up the steps to the front door of Fowler Crest. "Do me a favor and don't wreck it," she said.

Jessica gave her a thumbs-up sign. "I'll do my best," she replied airily. She blew Lila a kiss and shot down the driveway.

As she drove back into town, she wondered just how much time she would have to spend handing out leaflets on recycling. It didn't sound exactly thrilling. She was hoping she could convince Keith that it was a perfect beach day. She was pretty confident about her powers of persuasion, so she was smiling cheerfully when she pulled into the Dairi-Burger parking lot.

Keith was waiting for her. He had had to take a bus to Sweet Valley, since it would have taken him too long to bike there from Palisades. He and Jessica had agreed to meet at the Dairi-Burger. Now he jogged over, hoisting a bulging knapsack onto one shoulder.

"Hi," he said, opening the door and getting into the car.

"Hi yourself." Jessica gave him a big smile. "What's in the pack?"

Keith reached inside and pulled out a sheet of paper. "The flyers. The best thing to do is go to one of the big housing developments where there is a concentration of houses. We split up and take opposite sides of the street, handing them out if people are home, or else stuffing mailboxes."

"Split up?" Jessica repeated. "That doesn't sound very friendly."

Startled, Keith turned to look at her. "But we have to distribute all of these today," he said in a mystified tone.

"I was just kidding," Jessica said hastily. She pulled out of the parking lot. Obviously, bringing Keith around to her way of thinking was going to take a little longer than she had expected.

"Most of the girls I know wouldn't be willing to do this," he said, giving her a warm smile. "I think you're really great."

Jessica felt a shiver of delight. Everything Keith said he said with conviction and sincerity. Feeling flattered, she shrugged. "I believe in it, that's all."

"Terrific." Keith looked at her intently, and Jessica began to wonder if he was about to say something romantic. "Let's start on this street," he said at last.

Jessica blinked, thrown off balance. She was mentally prepared for a thrilling encounter, but Keith was watching road signs. With a sigh, she turned into Granada Estates and looked for a place to park.

"Here, you take this bunch," Keith said, scooping a handful of recycling flyers out of his knapsack. He stared into her eyes. "Be sure to tell people they're printed on one hundred percent recycled paper."

Jessica nodded solemnly, returning his mesmerizing look. His powers of persuasion were even stronger than her own! "I will," she said in a husky voice.

With a burst of energy and determination, Jessica strode up the sidewalk to the first house on her side of the street. She knocked on the door.

"Hi," she said when a white-haired man opened the door. "I have a little brochure here about recycling. Maybe you'd like to take a look

43

at it when you have a chance." She held it out invitingly.

He regarded her with suspicion. "Are you collecting money?" he growled.

"Nope!" she replied perkily. "Just giving out information."

"I'm not interested," the man said. He shut the door.

Indignant, Jessica stormed away. Across the street, Keith was talking earnestly with a man in jogging clothes. He saw her and waved.

Jessica gave him a big smile. Then she glared at the fistful of recycling brochures she held. The sooner they were distributed, the sooner they could go do something else. With a quick glance across the street, Jessica crammed four brochures into one mailbox. Then she plastered a big, friendly smile on her face and went to knock on the next door.

By the time Cara and Steven got back to the car, Cara was shaken up. She couldn't remember when Steven had been so distant and short-tempered. Everything she said seemed to rub him the wrong way.

I guess that just happens sometimes, she thought.

She sent Steven an apologetic smile as he backed the car up and pulled out of the parking lot. He still looked tense and withdrawn.

"Are you sure you don't want to go to the Dairi-Burger tonight?" she asked him, trying to make peace and cajole him into a better mood. "Everyone will be there."

"Look," Steven said gruffly, "sometimes I don't like to be with everyone. Besides, I told you I have to do some studying tonight."

Cara turned to stare out the window. "I'm sorry if everything I say makes you mad," she muttered.

"What?"

She shrugged. "Nothing."

There was no point in making a big deal out of it, she decided. It would probably be better just to be agreeable for the rest of the ride. She didn't want him to think she was nagging him.

"Sometime, let's rent all the James Bond movies at the video store and have a Bondathon," she suggested lightly. She watched his profile as he drove. "Wouldn't that be fun?" she prompted when he didn't answer.

Steven signaled for a right turn and pulled out onto the highway. "Yeah, I guess so."

Cara watched him silently for a moment. She

was beginning to get angry herself. "What's with you? You love the old Bond movies."

"We watch movies all the time!" Steven snapped. "Can't you think of anything else to do?"

Shocked, Cara turned around on the seat to face him squarely. "We do not watch movies *all* the time, Steven. What is wrong with you today?"

"Nothing," Steven answered irritably. "Nothing's wrong with me."

Cara frowned. "Well, you sure are acting like it. If something is bothering you, just say so!"

He looked out his window and muttered something.

"What?" Cara asked.

"I said nothing is bothering me," Steven replied in a condescendingly patient tone.

Cara's stomach did a flip-flop. She couldn't understand why he was in such a bad mood, and if he refused to talk about it, there was nothing she could do. She was hurt that he would speak to her so sarcastically. She racked her memory for something she might have done or said to make him act this way, but she couldn't remember anything. The possibility that he was tired of their relationship loomed over her like a dark cloud. Blinking back tears, Cara slumped into her seat.

Steven was silent, too. He was driving with a grim scowl on his face. He stared straight ahead without looking anywhere else. Cara noticed the speedometer was creeping up past sixty-five. She gulped. If they were pulled over for speeding, it would only aggravate the situation. That was definitely something to avoid.

"Steve," she said nervously. She was afraid he would snap at her again. "Don't forget, there are speed traps around here pretty often."

He didn't say anything, but he eased up on the gas pedal. After a few more minutes of silence, he let out a sigh.

"Listen, I'm sorry I've been such a grouch today," he said in a tired voice. He looked over at her and managed a smile. "I guess I'm thinking about my paper. You know, it's about seventy-five percent of my grade in that course. It has to be good."

Cara was so glad he was talking again that she smiled in relief. Maybe that really was all it was. "That's OK," she said gently. "I understand."

When they pulled up in front of Cara's apartment house, Steven cut the engine. He put his arm across her shoulders and pulled her to him. Cara rested her cheek against his chest, glad to be quiet and together.

But Steven pulled away after just a moment. "I'll call you," he said, kissing her lightly on her cheek.

Cara searched his eyes for something more, something that said everything was fine and back to normal. But he seemed so far away. Her heart sank.

"OK, bye," she whispered, sliding out.

She slammed the door and stood on the sidewalk while he drove away. She felt absolutely terrible.

She turned slowly and went inside. Maybe Jessica would know what the problem was.

Five

At four-thirty, Jessica was out in the backyard by the pool, struggling through an article on rain forest destruction. The slick magazine pages kept slipping between her fingers, which were oily with suntan lotion.

"Why don't those Brazilian people just quit cutting the trees down?" she asked out loud. "It's simple—just make them stop it."

She didn't see what all the controversy was about, but it was something Keith was passionately interested in. Jessica was hoping that he would become passionately interested in her, too. Reading up on boring subjects like oil exploration and acid rain was her way of making sure he would. Once he was hooked, maybe she could get him involved in something more interesting, like playing tennis, partying, and hanging out at the beach. After spending three hours handing out flyers, she thought it was *her* turn to plan their next date.

Prince Albert, the family's golden Labrador retriever, padded over, dropped a tennis ball into Jessica's lap and gave her a hopeful look. Jessica tossed the ball into the pool, then skimmed the photo captions in the article. Prince Albert splashed noisily after the ball.

"What a bore," Jessica muttered.

The cordless phone beside her lounge chair let out an electronic *breeep!* She snatched it up and pulled out the antenna.

"Hello?" she asked. She was hoping it would be Keith.

"Jess? It's Cara."

Jessica slumped. "Oh. Hi, Cara. What's up?" She flicked the pages back and forth, wishing the article didn't have to be so long and de-tailed.

"Well . . ." Cara hesitated. "I was wonder-ing. Do you know if—"

Jessica screamed as Prince Albert stopped next

to her and began shaking the water out of his fur. "Get away, Prince!" she yelled.

"Jessica?"

"Hi, sorry, what?" she asked.

"I said, do you know if anything's been bothering Steve?" Cara asked.

"Steve?" Jessica grimaced. "What could be wrong with him? You should be asking if anything's wrong with *me*, though."

"Why?"

Jessica tossed her wet magazine away and sighed dramatically. "Well, for starters, my parents are turning into total workaholics. They both work all the time, and I'm the one who gets stuck having to do everything at home. Cook dinner, do the laundry, wait around for the electrician, stuff like that. It's like I'm the only responsible person in this whole family." She closed her eyes in self-pity. "It's just not fair."

"Oh, I know what you mean," Cara said absently.

Jessica frowned. Usually Cara was so sympathetic, but at the moment, she didn't seem as if she was really listening very carefully.

"I'm serious," Jessica stressed. "Plus, the Fiat is still a terminal case, and no one will ever let me borrow a car. It's not like I go out all the time, but I do have social obligations, you know."

"Right," Cara said. She sighed into the phone.

"Like today," Jessica went on. She pushed her sunglasses up with one finger. "I was planning to go out with this guy Keith, right? Did I tell you about him? He's so gorgeous, Cara, and he's really involved in all this environmental and political stuff."

"Jess?" Cara interrupted. "Is Steve there?"

Taken aback, Jessica stared at the telephone. It wasn't like Cara to be so rude. "He just left a little while ago, all duded up. Wasn't he going to pick you up?"

There was a short pause. "Um, no, I—" Cara cleared her throat. "No, we're not going out tonight. He said he had to work on his project."

Jessica shrugged. "Well, I don't know where he was going. Anyway, this guy Keith asked me to help him hand out these flyers about recycling today, right? So all I wanted to do was borrow Mom's car, but no. She had to use it for work today. Then Dad gets all mad and says if she's going to work all day, so is he, so he takes his car and goes to *his* office—"

"Hey, Jessica?" Cara broke in again. "Look, I have to go, OK?"

"Oh. All right," Jessica replied haughtily. "Goodbye."

When she hung up, Jessica sat frowning into space for a moment. Sometimes Cara could be *so* insensitive.

Then a thought dawned on her. If Steven wasn't going out with Cara, where was he going?

Steven and Andrea strolled through the aquarium, deep in conversation. Andrea told Steven how the luminous tanks of fish and coral reminded her of paintings she had seen, or dreams she had had. Steven couldn't take his eyes off her face. In the underwater light, she looked more like Tricia than ever. The only thing that bothered him was that she had her hair pinned up on top of her head. He preferred it down, the way Tricia had always worn hers. But that was a minor detail. It wasn't important.

"I love it here," Andrea said as they stepped out into the late afternoon sunshine.

Steven nodded, entranced by his memories

and by Andrea. "Me, too." He nodded to the left. "Come on, let's go see the otters."

"Oh! Great idea—I love otters!" Andrea said with a happy smile.

"I knew you would," Steven replied.

Tricia had loved watching the playful animals, too. The two of them had spent many happy Saturday afternoons at the aquarium, walking hand-in-hand, feeding the seals, and just watching the fish. Bringing Andrea there brought back so many memories for Steven that he thought he would cry. But he was happy and peaceful, too.

"Look at that one, swimming on its back." Andrea laughed and pointed into the otter pool. "Isn't it beautiful?"

Steven was looking at her as he nodded. "Yes."

Even though she didn't turn to face him, Andrea obviously knew what he meant. "Wouldn't it be wonderful to be that carefree?" she went on in a casual tone. She leaned her arms on the railing and looked down into the water. "There's something so joyful and uninhibited about them."

Steven finally turned to look at the otters.

That was just the kind of remark Tricia would have made, he thought happily. The way the otters glided through the water so smoothly and effortlessly reminded him of the hang gliders he had seen in the canyons. He glanced at Andrea. He was positive she would react differently than Cara had done if he told her about his new interest.

"You know what they make me think of?" he began, watching Andrea's face.

She lifted her eyebrows. "What?"

"Flying," he said.

Andrea smiled. "That's true! It's very similar. Wouldn't it be fantastic to be able to fly like a bird?"

"Hang gliding would be like that," Steven pointed out. He felt as though he were testing her. It felt sneaky, but he couldn't help it. He had to know if she would react the way he thought she would.

A half-scared, half-laughing expression came into Andrea's eyes. "I'd be scared to death to try that," she admitted, shaking her head. "But you're right, it's probably the closest thing to flying humans can do."

Steven felt a surge of elation. He had known

she would feel that way! He couldn't stop smiling. Impulsively, he put out his hand and unclipped the barrette holding up Andrea's hair. Her strawberry-blond curls cascaded around her shoulders.

"Hey!" She let out a startled laugh. "What are you doing?"

"Your hair looks so pretty loose," Steven told her. He grinned disarmingly. "I just couldn't resist."

Andrea tipped her head to one side. "Oh, yeah?" She smiled and held her hand out for the barrette. When he gave it back to her, she began to gather her hair to pin it up again.

"Couldn't you leave it down for a while?" Steven asked wistfully.

"You really mean it, don't you?" She shook her head with a wondering smile. She shrugged and put the barrette in her purse. "OK."

Steven drew a deep breath. "Thanks. Are you hungry? Do you want to get hamburgers and eat on the beach?"

"Sure," Andrea agreed. "That sounds good."

Andrea was everything Tricia had been, Steven decided jubilantly. And everything Cara was *not*. Andrea was so much like Tricia, it was just like finding Tricia all over again. It was a miracle. He couldn't find her again and then just let her walk out of his life. He couldn't.

"Let's get ice cream first," Andrea said, interrupting Steven's thoughts. "My motto is, life is uncertain, so eat dessert first."

Steven laughed. "That's an excellent philosophy. Two chocolate cones, coming up."

"Make mine vanilla, please," Andrea corrected him as they reached the ice-cream vendor.

"Vanilla?" Steven echoed in surprise. "But—"

Just in time, he stopped himself from saying, "Tricia always had chocolate." He stared at Andrea, at a loss for words.

"Isn't vanilla allowed?" Andrea said lightly, but Steven thought he saw a look of uncertainty cross her face.

"Sure. No problem," Steven said with difficulty.

It didn't matter if Andrea liked a different kind of ice cream, he realized. What mattered was that in every other way, Andrea was just like Tricia. And he wasn't going to lose her again.

When Steven got home, his parents were watching TV in the living room. They both looked very tired and gloomy in the flickering light.

"Hi, Mom. Hi, Dad," Steven said, perching on the arm of an easy chair. "What's on?"

"Some dumb thing," Alice Wakefield replied. "How was your date?"

"Great." Steven felt slightly dishonest; he knew his parents assumed he had gone out with Cara. But he couldn't help feeling wonderful. Being with Andrea was just like old times.

"Listen," he went on. "There's this hang-gliding club that has an orientation meeting every Sunday morning. I'm going to check it out tomorrow."

"Hang gliding?" his father asked. He looked surprised. "I didn't know you were interested in hang gliding."

Steven shrugged. "It's something I just decided to try," he said. "It looks like fun."

Mrs. Wakefield was pressing her lips together and frowning. "Steve, I don't know about this," she began in a doubtful voice.

"What do you mean?" Steven asked. He knew exactly what she meant, though. Ever since Elizabeth had been in a motorcycle accident, Mrs. Wakefield had been very apprehensive about any of them taking up activities that seemed dangerous. She was already upset.

"Honey, I know you're old enough to make your own decisions," she continued.

"So let him make them," Mr. Wakefield cut in. "He's a big boy, Alice."

She gave him an irritated look. "Ned, I just want him to know how I feel about it."

"No, what you want him to do is feel guilty about worrying you and *not* do it," Mr. Wakefield replied. He looked at Steven. "My opinion is, go for it while you have the chance. It won't be long before you can't afford to take any risks at all," he said bitterly.

Steven felt slightly sick as he listened to his parents. He had never heard his father sound so hard and cynical before. It was a little frightening. His parents had always been so easygoing and reliable, and so affectionate with each other.

"I'd like to know what you mean by that," Alice Wakefield said to her husband. She sounded hurt, but she raised her chin defiantly while she looked at him.

He looked at the television and sighed. "He's young. He doesn't have any obligations to get in his way. That's all I'm saying. If he wants some adventure, I say he should be able to have it."

"Listen," Steven cut in anxiously. "I'm not even a hundred percent sure I'll do it, Mom. I just want to check it out. Besides, it's pretty expensive."

"See?" Mr. Wakefield said with a humorless laugh. "He's already backing off. Good work, Alice."

Mrs. Wakefield folded her arms. "I'm your mother, Steven. It's natural for me to be *concerned*. That's all I'm saying. But if you want to try it, I don't want to get in your way."

"How expensive, Steve?" Mr. Wakefield asked.

Steven avoided his mother's eyes. "Well. . . ."

"Listen, I'll lend you the money," his father said. "I really think you should do it."

"Ned!" Mrs. Wakefield sounded shocked. "I don't think—" She cut herself off and glared at her husband.

Steven swallowed hard, and looked from his mother to his father and back again. "Well, OK," he stammered, feeling uncertain and concerned. "Thanks, Dad. I'll let you know how I like it."

When neither of them said anything more, Steven stood up and left the room. Compared to being with Andrea, coming home was pretty unpleasant. It only made him want to be with her even more.

He began to smile as he thought of things he and Andrea could do together in the coming week. He couldn't wait to see her again. By the time he got to his room, he was whistling happily.

Six

Jessica hurried up the steps to City Hall on Wednesday evening to meet Keith. He had asked her to meet him at a public hearing on whether the city needed a trash incinerator. It sounded pretty miserable, but Jessica was still willing to give Keith the benefit of the doubt.

She had to push her way past a group of demonstrators carrying placards that read "Get Your Ash Out of My Town!" and "Smoke Gets In Your Eyes." A local TV news crew was videotaping them, and Jessica paused long enough to send the camera a bright smile. Then she went inside and found the auditorium.

"Jessica!" Keith waved to her from a seat in the front row. "I'm up here."

Jessica returned his wave. Inwardly, though, she cringed. He was dressed in an outfit that must have come from the thrift shop. And knowing his sentiments about recycling and waste, his old corduroys and work shirt probably *were* from the secondhand store. Jessica looked down at her crisp jeans and silk T-shirt and shrugged. *We can't all be great dressers*, she thought matter-of-factly.

"You made it! Great!" he said as she sat down next to him.

She smiled. "I made it. So . . ." She looked around curiously. She wasn't really sure what went on at a public hearing. Up at the front podium, she saw someone she recognized. "That's Mr. Santelli," she said, pointing him out to Keith. "Maria Santelli is in my class at school."

Keith narrowed his eyes. "He's the city planning commissioner," he said in a suspicious voice. "He's probably pushing the incinerator proposal."

"Oh, yeah." Jessica bit her lip. She guessed that Keith's tone meant he was *against* the incinerator. "I hope it goes down in flames," she hazarded.

"Me, too," Keith agreed.

Relieved, Jessica sat back and let her breath out.

"Burning garbage is such a total waste of time," Keith said, frowning at her earnestly. "It just ignores the real issue of why there *is* so much garbage."

Jessica nodded, looking into his eyes. She wondered when he was going to notice *her* the way she had noticed *him*. "I know what you mean," she said softly.

"I mean, the problem isn't just going to go away!" Keith went on. He clenched his fists. "We have to conserve and recycle, not just find new ways of throwing out the trash."

Jessica was torn between boredom and interest. On one hand, Keith was so sincere and passionate about the issues that she couldn't help feeling attracted to him. But on the other hand, she only wished he could be passionate about something besides garbage—her, for instance. She suppressed a sigh.

"Do you think we could go somewhere afterward?" she suggested as the moderator banged the gavel. The room hushed. "To get something to eat?"

Keith nodded, his eyes on the podium. "Sure, how about the Whole Earth Café?" he whispered.

Ugh, Jessica said to herself.

"What do they serve?" she asked, leaning close enough to whisper in his ear. She noticed the way his dark hair curled just behind his ear.

Keith turned to look at her. Their eyes met, and even though they were in a room full of people, Jessica thought it was very romantic. His lips parted. "They have natural vegetable juices and mineral water," he said huskily.

"Really?" Jessica breathed, gazing into his eyes. "That sounds delicious."

"Will the meeting now come to order!" Mr. Santelli called out. He shuffled some papers together. "We have a lot to get through tonight. We have several experts here who can answer your questions. There are three people in the audience with microphones. If you raise your hand to be recognized, the nearest one will bring you a mike."

Very quickly, people began asking questions about the trash incinerator. Everyone wanted to be sure it would not be in his or her neighborhood if it was built. A number of people were worried about toxic fumes. Keith listened intently to everything that was said.

But Jessica was bored to death. She wished she had a magazine or something to read, but even more, she wished they could leave. It was hard to believe Keith wasn't interested in anything but saving the world. The sooner they got around to the things she liked to do—go dancing, hang out at the Dairi-Burger—the better. She put her hand over her mouth to hide a yawn, but when Keith glanced her way, she changed it into a smile.

"This is really interesting," she whispered to him.

He nodded. "It sure is."

Sighing, Jessica slumped into her seat and prepared herself for a long wait.

On Friday, Todd met Elizabeth outside her math class. It was lunchtime, and although he couldn't have lunch with her that day, Todd walked Elizabeth to the cafeteria. Hand in hand, they let the crowds hurry past them. Elizabeth sighed heavily and shook her head at her private thoughts.

"What is it?" Todd asked.

Elizabeth looked up at him. "Oh . . . I just feel so—" She frowned. "It's my parents," she finally said.

Todd tipped his head to one side and gave her a concerned look. "What about them?"

"I don't know." Elizabeth shrugged. "They're arguing all the time now. They never used to be like this! It really makes me feel awful."

"Is something in particular bothering them?"

Elizabeth shook her head. "I just don't know. How can you ask about something like that, though?" Her voice caught, and she looked away. She thought she might cry.

Todd squeezed her hand. "Come on, Liz. It probably isn't that bad. They work hard—maybe it's just pressure building up. They haven't had a vacation in a long time, and they're just taking it out on each other."

"That's true," Elizabeth said. She wanted to believe that pressure and tension were all it was. "Maybe I'm just blowing it out of proportion."

They stopped outside the cafeteria, and Todd looked into her eyes. "Liz, every relationship has ups and downs. You know that. Just try not to get too worried about this. It'll blow over."

Elizabeth nodded slowly. The love and concern she saw in Todd's eyes made her feel much better. Resting her cheek against his chest, she asked, "Why do you have to be so nice all the time?"

Todd chuckled as he wrapped his arms around

her. "That's just the way I am—an incredibly wonderful person."

"Right." Elizabeth smiled and sniffed hard. "OK. I'll stop acting paranoid about it," she promised.

He touched her cheek. "If you want to talk about it, you know where to go." He grinned. "To Enid."

Elizabeth punched him in the arm. "Thanks a lot for nothing." She laughed.

"No problem." Todd held up a lunch bag. "Lucky me, getting to have lunch with Mr. Collins and talk about my English paper," he said. "I'd better get going. I'll see you later, OK?"

"Bye." Elizabeth smiled warmly and watched him stroll back down the hall. Todd could always make her feel loved and secure.

But as soon as he was out of sight, her worries came crowding back in on her. She tried to suppress them as she walked into the noisy lunchroom. She took a tray and walked slowly past that day's cafeteria selections. Nothing appealed to her. At last she put a ham and cheese sandwich and a glass of milk on her tray. She paid for her food, then paused to scan the crowd, looking for some friends to sit with.

"Liz!"

She turned at the sound of her name. Cara was beckoning to her from a nearby table. Elizabeth felt her heart sink. The last person she wanted to talk to was Cara, but she couldn't turn away now. Trying to look cheerful, Elizabeth went to join her brother's girlfriend.

"Hi, Cara," she said, putting her tray on the table and sitting down across from the other girl.

Cara gave her a tired smile. "Hi. What's up?"

"Not much," Elizabeth answered. She could see by Cara's expression that she was just waiting to ask about Steven. Elizabeth dreaded it, but there was no way to avoid the subject.

"Could I ask you something, Liz?" Cara asked the next moment.

Elizabeth knew what Cara was going to ask. Just one look at the girl was enough to see that she was depressed and worried.

And Elizabeth knew exactly why Cara was so upset. Steven had gone out with Andrea several times during the past week. That couldn't have left any time for Cara. Knowing Steven, he was probably insisting to her that nothing was wrong. But Elizabeth knew that when a person was close to someone else, that person could always tell when something was wrong. Cara definitely knew something was up, and it was obviously tearing her apart.

"Sure," Elizabeth said. She avoided meeting Cara's eyes.

Cara fiddled with her soda straw. "I was wondering, do you know if Steve is upset about something lately? I mean"—she laughed hollowly—"usually he tells me everything, but he's been kind of busy. I just thought you might know what it could be."

Anger at Steven suddenly filled Elizabeth. He was hurting a warm, loving girl by lying to her and cheating on her. It wasn't right. But there was nothing she could do. She had promised she wouldn't tell anyone about Andrea, and she wasn't at all happy with that burden.

"Well, you know this independent study thing he's doing is a lot of work," Elizabeth said. She felt like a liar. "He really is doing a lot of research for that."

Cara nodded. She was looking down at her lap, ripping a paper napkin into little pieces. "Yeah, he told me how important it is."

"And—" Elizabeth searched for something to say that was true. "Also, he's been taking hang-gliding lessons. He really likes it."

71

"He does?" Cara whispered. "I didn't know he was actually doing it."

Elizabeth's heart ached with pity and anger. Steven hadn't even told Cara that he had started the lessons. He was being a jerk, she thought. He was throwing away a wonderful relationship for a ghost. Elizabeth was positive Steven saw Andrea only as a replacement for Tricia. He was deceiving Cara, he was deceiving Andrea, and most of all, he was deceiving himself.

"You don't think there's something else?" Cara asked. She stared at Elizabeth pleadingly. "We can't even talk without having it turn into an argument. I don't know what's wrong!"

A sick feeling settled in Elizabeth's stomach as she realized that that was just what was going on between her parents. She wondered frantically if her father had become interested in another woman. Elizabeth forced herself to respond to Cara.

"No, I don't know, Cara," she said hoarsely. "You'll have to talk to him about it, I guess." Elizabeth knew she couldn't sit there any longer, lying for Steven and worrying about her parents at the same time. She scraped her chair back abruptly. "I just remembered something. I have to go. Sorry."

Without waiting for Cara to answer, Elizabeth hurried away. She had totally lost her appetite. After putting her tray on the conveyor belt, she hurried out of the cafeteria. She was so upset that she collided head-on with her twin at the door.

"Whoa, Liz." Jessica laughed. She looked at her twin sister. "What's up?"

Lila Fowler was with Jessica. She gave Elizabeth a speculative look. Lila was always on the prowl for gossip.

"Nothing's up. I have to go, Jess. See you later."

When Elizabeth was gone, Jessica looked at Lila and raised her eyebrows. "Teenage panic," she quipped. "She probably has to brush her hair."

"Right, Jessica." Lila giggled. "Liz is such a slave to fashion."

Jessica grinned. "This is true. Hey, there's Cara. Come on."

Jessica followed Lila to the table and flopped down across from Cara. She waited for Cara to say hello, but her friend didn't even look up. Finally, Jessica said, "You can smile now, we're here."

"Hi, you guys," Cara muttered. She jabbed

her straw into her soda and took a long sip. She hardly seemed to notice their presence.

Jessica and Lila exchanged a look. They were both thinking the same thing, Jessica was sure. Cara had been a real bore lately. She was always absent-minded and down in the dumps, and she hardly said a word.

Thinking about it, Jessica realized that Steven had been acting a bit strange recently, too. But if they were having problems with their relationship, Jessica thought, they should keep it to themselves. There was no reason for Cara to make everyone else depressed just because she and Steven were having some lovers' quarrel.

"Cara, do you want to go to the beach tomorrow?" Jessica asked.

Cara shrugged. "I don't know. Maybe."

"Well, don't be so excited about it," Lila said, fiddling with her gold bracelets. "You're really getting carried away."

Silently Cara raised her eyes and looked at them steadily. Jessica saw Cara's throat move up and down in a hard swallow.

"I just don't really feel very much like it, I guess," Cara said.

Jessica frowned. Maybe this was more serious than she had thought at first.

Lila propped her elbows on the table and stared at Cara. "Well, do you feel like going to the mall this afternoon? Come on, say yes," she urged when Cara began to shake her head.

"Yeah, come on, Cara," Jessica chimed in. "We could do makeovers on each other."

"Well . . ." Cara bit her lower lip.

"Listen," Lila said. She leaned forward and lowered her voice conspiratorially. "There's this dress I saw at the Unique Boutique—I want to try it on and see what you guys think. And I *really* need your opinion, Cara. So you have to come," she concluded with a grin. "And that pretty much settles that."

Cara drew a deep breath and managed to smile. "All right," she said. "I guess so."

Jessica sat back, satisfied. Now maybe things would get back to normal.

Seven

By the time Elizabeth got home from school on Friday, she was in a terrible mood. She dumped her books on the hall table and walked listlessly to the kitchen for a snack.

Steven looked up when she entered. He was studying at the kitchen table with Prince Albert at his feet.

"Hey, Liz," he said in a cheerful voice.

Elizabeth stared at her brother for a moment. The sight of him made her so angry that she couldn't speak. She turned away and opened the refrigerator. After a moment, she took out a brick of cheddar cheese and a container of apple juice. She didn't feel like getting into a discussion about anything. There was a good chance she would either yell or start crying if she did.

But Steven didn't notice the warning signs. "What's up? Is Sweet Valley High still the same as always?"

Elizabeth put the cheese and apple juice down carefully. "Why don't you ask your girlfriend? Cara Walker? Remember her? She's a nice girl, about my height? Dark hair and brown eyes?" Elizabeth stopped and steadily returned Steven's shocked stare.

An angry scowl wrinkled Steven's forehead, but he didn't say anything.

"Cara asked me today if you were upset about anything," Elizabeth went on. "I had to pretend I didn't know what she was talking about."

Steven cleared his throat. "Thanks," he muttered, rearranging his papers.

"That's not exactly what I was hoping you'd say."

"Well, what *do* you want me to say?" Steven asked gruffly. "Not that it's any of your business!"

"If Cara comes to me and asks me about you, and I have to lie to her, it *is* my business," Elizabeth retorted. She fought to control her voice. "Why are you doing this to her?"

He frowned. "I'm not doing anything to Cara. I haven't lied to her."

"No? What do you call it, then?" Elizabeth shook her head. "Steve, the girl is a wreck! She's so upset. She knows there's something you aren't telling her. You're not fooling anyone but yourself if you think she doesn't know. Why don't you just break up with her? At least that would be honest."

"I don't want to break up with her!" Steven exclaimed. "And I certainly don't want to hurt her. I know how it feels to be dumped, and I don't want to put her through that."

"But you're hurting her just as badly by cheating on her!" Elizabeth insisted.

The dog kept looking from one to the other with a concerned expression in his brown eyes. He wagged his tail hopefully, as if asking for peace.

Steven put his face in his hands and let out a heavy sigh. "It's not like that, Liz," he began.

"Yes, it is." Elizabeth felt tired and empty. She tried to keep her voice as sympathetic as possible, but it was very hard. What she really wanted was to take a nap and forget everything. "Steve, are you finished seeing Andrea or not?"

"Liz, you just don't understand," Steven began slowly. His face was still buried in his hands, and his words came out muffled. "Being with Andrea is so— She makes me feel like—" He couldn't finish.

Elizabeth shook her head. "You're right. I don't understand. You're obsessed with her, and it really makes me worry!"

"Oh, come on, Liz!" Steven replied. He looked at her and tried to smile. "You're exaggerating. I'm not *obsessed*."

Elizabeth just stared at him silently. She didn't think she was exaggerating at all. Steven looked away.

"Listen, I just—" Steven broke off as the back door opened.

Alice Wakefield came in, loaded down with a stack of wallpaper books and a grocery bag. She heaved everything onto the counter.

"Hi, Mom," Elizabeth said. She was glad for the interruption. The argument with Steven was getting to be too upsetting. She didn't even want to talk about it, but she couldn't stop thinking about Cara. As long as she knew her brother was hurting Cara, Elizabeth couldn't keep silent.

"Hi, kids," Alice Wakefield replied. She looked

utterly frazzled. "This client is just making me crazy. She wants to choose wallpaper *tonight*."

"But it's Friday!" Steven pointed out indignantly.

Mrs. Wakefield rolled her eyes. "I noticed. Honestly, sometimes I wonder why I let myself get used this way. People can be so inconsiderate."

Elizabeth felt sorry for her mother. Normally Mrs. Wakefield loved her job, loved talking about it, loved to share her successes with the family. But at the moment she was acting as though her career were controlling her instead of the other way around.

"Do you want me to make dinner?" Elizabeth offered.

Mrs. Wakefield gave her a grateful smile. "Thanks, sweetie. I appreciate it." She glanced at her watch. "And if you could call your dad—"

She broke off. There was an awkward silence. None of them looked at the others.

"No. I'll do it," Mrs. Wakefield decided and reached for the wall phone. After dialing the number, she waited, tapping her foot nervously. "Hi, Marge? It's Alice, is Ned in? Thanks."

Elizabeth stole a quick glance at her brother. For the moment, she didn't care about his problems with Andrea and Cara. She just hoped that she would hear her mother talking to her father in a kind, loving way.

"Hi, Ned. Mrs. Rappaport is on the warpath again. I have to work tonight, but Liz is getting dinner." Mrs. Wakefield paused, listening. "No, I didn't have time, Ned—"

Elizabeth's stomach sank. Prince Albert whined to go out, but nobody moved.

"Then why don't *you* call him?" Alice said in a tight voice. "You're the one who wanted to know. I don't even know why you asked me to make the call." She sighed wearily. "Of course I realize you have a full schedule. So do I."

Suddenly Alice Wakefield seemed to become aware of Elizabeth and Steven, sitting like stones at the table. She put one hand over her eyes and drew a deep breath. "Ned, let's not talk about this now. I have to take a shower and leave. OK. I'll see you when I get home—I don't know, maybe eight or eight-thirty. Bye."

When she hung up the phone, their mother looked at them. She was frowning, and she seemed to be trying to find the right words. She started to say something, but just shook her head and hurried out of the room.

Elizabeth tried to swallow the painful lump in her throat. She felt as if everything she had ever known was suddenly different and unstable.

"What is going on?" Steven whispered.

"I don't know," Elizabeth replied dejectedly. "I wish I did."

Cara held back a sigh as Jessica blended eyeshadow on her lids. The department store's makeup counter was quiet for a Friday afternoon, and Jessica, Cara, and Lila were going wild with the samples. Or at least Jessica and Lila were going wild. Cara was just putting up with it, since she had nothing else to do except sit at home worrying about Steven.

"This mocha is such a hot color on you," Jessica said gleefully. She stood back for a critical look. "What do you think, Li?"

Lila pursed her lips, admiring the cherry-red lip gloss she had tried on. She glanced at Cara. "She looks like you gave her a black eye, Jessica."

"Oh, great," Cara groaned. "That's all I need." She grabbed a tissue from the box on the counter and wiped the shadow from her eyelids. Her reflection in the mirror stared back at her: she looked like she was wiping away tears.

"You guys, I'm sick of this," she announced, crumpling the stained tissue into a ball.

Lila heaved a patient sigh. "OK, Cara. Whatever you say."

"What about that dress you wanted us to review for you, Lila?" Jessica looked in the mirror and adjusted a strand of her honey-gold hair. "Maybe it would look good on me—I'm going out with Keith tonight, and I think I need a secret weapon."

"Right—it's at the Unique Boutique," Lila said, laughing. "Follow me, you guys."

Cara realized she had made a big mistake by coming to the mall with her friends. She knew she was acting like a lead weight and that they were probably fed up with her. She decided to take the bus home if they weren't ready to go soon.

She was following Jessica and Lila listlessly, not even looking where she was going. But once they entered the store, Cara looked up.

Then she felt her heart jolt. Tricia Martin was standing behind the counter. Cara looked wildly over at Jessica and Lila, but they were busy talking and hadn't noticed. Cara turned to look again.

It wasn't Tricia, of course, Cara saw with

relief. In fact, at a second glance the resemblance wasn't as strong as she had first thought. The salesclerk's general appearance was like Tricia's, and her features were similar. But her eyes were different, and the way she gestured and moved was a bit different, too.

That is weird, though, she told herself in amazement.

She walked over to her friends, who were examining a dress, presumably the one Lila was interested in buying. "Look at that girl," she whispered, nodding toward the counter. "Does she remind you guys of anyone in particular?"

They followed her gaze. "Hey, you're right," Jessica said. "She looks a little bit like that actress, Betty Garrett."

Cara frowned. "No, someone else."

Lila suddenly gasped. "You're right! Tricia Martin!" she hissed.

"Hey, I see what you mean," Jessica added. "Wow, I haven't thought about her in a long time."

Cara nodded. "At first I thought it was actually her! But she doesn't look *that* much like her when you really take a good look."

"Why would you want to take a good look

anyway?" Lila said snottily. "She's just a sales-clerk."

"Really," Jessica agreed. "Hey, look at this dress," she went on.

While Jessica and Lila hunted through the racks, Cara drifted closer to the counter. She pretended to be looking at the racks of clothes, too, but she kept glancing at the girl who resembled Tricia. Now she was marking sale prices on some fancy barrettes.

Cara stepped up to the counter and began picking through a display of silk scarves. She couldn't get over the coincidence.

A button on the wall telephone started flashing. A moment later, a discreet *bing-bing* sounded. The girl picked up the receiver. "Unique Boutique."

A wide smile spread across her face when she recognized the caller's voice. "Hi!" she said brightly. "No, it's not too busy right now. I'm just doing some labels." She crossed out another price while she listened, and then nodded. "Oh, that's terrible. What are they fighting about?"

Cara knew she should walk away. But something held her there. Maybe it was being reminded of someone Steven had loved so much.

"Sure, that was fun. I really had a good time. No," she said, laughing. "No, you would *never* get me up in one of those things. I told you I'd be terrified." She paused again and let out another laugh. "I'll leave the hang gliding to you."

Cara felt a jet of adrenalin shoot through her all the way to her fingertips. Her hand froze on one of the scarves, and her gaze was fixed blindly on the girl's profile. *It has to be a coincidence*, she told herself in panic. *It has to be.*

"The aquarium again? Tonight? I thought you were going to get some work done on that legal ethics study." The girl frowned and hesitated before she answered. "All right. I have to work until six o'clock, but you could pick me up here at five after or so."

Steven loved the aquarium. Steven was working on a legal ethics study. But it had to be a coincidence. It *had* to be!

"Cara? Come here a second!" Lila called.

Cara couldn't move.

"OK, Steve. See you later." The girl hung up.

Tears of anguish filled Cara's eyes. She turned and stumbled into Jessica.

"What's wrong, Cara?" Jessica asked.

Shaking her head, Cara pushed past her friend and ran out of the store. Now she knew what was bothering Steven, why he wasn't communicating, why he was so busy! Steven had found another Tricia Martin, and now there was no room for Cara Walker in his life.

Cara didn't even care that people were staring at her and her tear-streaked face. She raced out of the mall and flagged down a bus just as it was pulling away from the main entrance. After she climbed on board, the bus lurched away and Cara staggered to the back, sank into a seat, and cried from the bottom of her heart.

Eight

Cara woke up with a dull headache from crying herself to sleep. At first she couldn't remember why she felt so miserable.

And then it all came flooding back. With a groan, she rolled over and buried her pounding head underneath the pillow.

For a few minutes, Cara gave in to hopelessness. Losing Steven would hurt more than anything in the world. Just thinking about it brought tears to her eyes.

But gradually she came to her senses. *Maybe it's not too late*, she thought. Maybe there was still time to salvage the relationship. There might not be that much damage done yet.

Cara sat up, rubbed her eyes, and tried to concentrate. The most important thing was to stay calm, she decided. If she gave in to panic or despair she knew she would never win.

In the cool morning light, Cara took a long hard look at the facts. All she knew was that Steven had found someone who reminded him of Tricia Martin. She deduced that he had seen the girl several times already. That explained why he had been so distant and preoccupied.

But he has to know he'll never have another Tricia, Cara thought.

She clenched her jaw as she ran over all the things she needed to say to Steven. She would tell him in all honesty that she could understand and sympathize with him. She knew as well as anybody did how much he had loved Tricia Martin. Cara had to convince him she was on his side, that she appreciated how surprised and glad he must have been to see "Tricia" again.

But you can't live in the past, Cara said to him in her imagination. If she stayed calm, reasonable, and kind, wouldn't he realize that she was the one who loved him now?

It couldn't be too late!

For the next twenty minutes, Cara paced back

and forth across her tiny bedroom, rehearsing all the wise and loving things she would say to Steven. He would agree with her that their relationship was important and worth saving. He *would*.

Finally, Cara squared her shoulders and picked up the telephone. She paused as she made a silent wish for everything to be fine, and then dialed.

"Hello?" Steven's voice was hopeful and bright.

Cara drew a deep breath. "Hi, it's Cara," she said casually, as though she weren't scared to death.

There was a pause. *He's disappointed. He was hoping it would be her*, Cara realized, her heart pounding rapidly.

"I have to talk to you," Cara said. She took a deep breath to calm herself. "It's important."

"Go ahead," Steven replied. He sounded far away. "What's up?"

Cara tried to make her voice behave. She squeezed her eyes shut and said, "I was at the mall yesterday. I went to the Unique Boutique."

There was a weighty silence on the other end of the line.

"I know how you must feel," Cara rushed

91

on. "I mean, I can see why you would want to go out with her, Steve, but I just think you shouldn't dwell in the past, you know what I mean?"

Cara could hear how strained and desperate she sounded. But Steven still didn't say anything. She fought back the rising tidal wave of panic.

"Steven?" she pleaded. "How long have you been seeing her? Are you going to keep seeing her? I mean, what's going on? Where do I fit in?" She realized her voice was rising, but she couldn't control it.

"What is this? Some kind of third degree?" Steven finally exploded in an angrily defensive tone. "And since when do you go around spying on me, anyway?"

Cara gasped and grabbed the phone cord tightly. "I wasn't spying on you! I was just there! I heard her talking to you on the phone!"

"So you admit you were deliberately listening?" Steven demanded.

Shocked, Cara said, "Steve! I couldn't help it! What was I supposed to do when I heard another girl making plans to go out with you? Just walk away?"

Cara pressed one hand across her mouth. It

wasn't coming out right at all! What had happened to all those things she had rehearsed? She tried to regain some of her composure.

"Look," she said, pitching her voice lower, "I don't want to sound like a witch. I just hope you aren't getting caught up in your memories of Tricia. That's why you went out with that girl, isn't it?"

Steven breathed heavily into the phone. "What about it?"

"Steven!" Cara said, blinking back tears. "Tricia is *dead!*" She bit her lip. As soon as the words were out, she regretted saying them.

"Don't you think I know that?" Steven said harshly.

Cara wiped away a tear with the back of her hand. "Steve, I'm sorry. I just don't understand what's happening to us! Don't I deserve some kind of explanation?"

"Yes, but you—" Steven broke off and swore under his breath. "Listen, Cara. I'm sorry you had to find out this way."

"Me, too!" Cara said shakily. "But what I want to know is, are you going to stop seeing her?"

"You don't understand!" Steven told her. "She's just like Tricia—"

Cara gulped. "Steven, she's *not*. She couldn't be! You must just be imagining that she is."

"What—you think I'm acting crazy? Is that it?" Steven demanded.

"No! I didn't say that!" Cara shot back. A wild mix of emotions tumbled through her: anger, pain, hurt, betrayal, love, despair. This was a nightmare.

"I just feel I deserve to know what's going on!" she said in a tightly controlled voice.

"You are so possessive, Cara—" Steven began.

"Possessive?" she echoed in disbelief. "How can you say that? You're supposed to be my *boyfriend!*"

Steven laughed bitterly. "Well, then, maybe that's the problem."

Cara's heart turned over. "What does that mean?" she whispered.

"Oh, come on." Steven sighed. "We both know, don't we, Cara?

"Fine," Cara said through gritted teeth. "I understand now. I guess that's it."

"I guess so," Steven agreed.

They were both silent. Cara knew she couldn't say another word, so she just hung up the phone. For several heartbeats, she sat there, shaking.

It was over.

Steven was stunned. *What just happened?* he asked himself.

His head was spinning. All along, he had thought he knew what he was doing. But now, without warning, everything seemed to be haywire, out of control.

"I didn't mean to break up with her," he said aloud still dazed.

But, maybe it was just as well, he decided the next minute. If he was really in love with Andrea . . . But he couldn't ignore the fact that he felt confused, lonely, and horribly ashamed of himself. He knew he had to talk to somebody.

He quickly picked up the phone again and began to dial Andrea's number. Then he felt a sting of guilt. He couldn't go that quickly from one girl to another. It wasn't right. It wasn't fair.

Just as he stood up, the door opened and Elizabeth looked in.

"Hi, Steve," she said. She had an apologetic look on her face.

Steven hoped she didn't see the tears in his eyes. "Hey, Liz."

"I just wanted to say I'm sorry about biting

your head off yesterday afternoon," Elizabeth told him. "I know you don't want to hurt anyone, and I know you're big enough to make your own decisions." She gave him a playful smile. "OK?"

For a moment, Steven was silent. The irony of the situation was unbelievable. Elizabeth's words cut like a knife. "OK," he mumbled at last, standing up quickly. He couldn't meet her eyes. "I have to go to my hang gliding lesson," he said.

He brushed past her without another word.

Jessica bit off the corner of her toast. "Keith was telling me last night about this fund drive he was part of to stop oil exploration in Alaska," she told her mother. "Can you believe most people didn't even care?" She rolled her eyes. "It's terrible."

"The truth is, most people only care about their own lives and their own immediate concerns," Mrs. Wakefield pointed out. She took a sip of her coffee. "That's just the way ninety percent of the world is."

Mr. Wakefield rustled the newspaper. "That's a pretty cynical attitude, Alice," he said.

"I'm just being realistic," she replied in a matter-of-fact way.

Jessica shrugged. "Well, Keith isn't like that at all. He believes in things, you know? Like he believes in a nuclear-free world. He even sat down in the road in front of a weapons plant once, can you believe it?" She closed her eyes. "He just gives me goosebumps."

"Are you sure those goosebumps aren't related to how cute he is?" Mrs. Wakefield teased.

Jessica gave her mother a stern look. "Positive, Mom. Give me some credit."

Mrs. Wakefield chuckled.

"Actually . . ." Jessica's father put the newspaper down and folded his arms thoughtfully. "I have to say, I have a lot of respect for your friend. I wish I had more to show for myself in that line. I haven't accomplished much of anything."

Mrs. Wakefield's eyes widened. "What do you mean? You work so hard for this family! You've built a very successful law practice. How can you say you've never accomplished anything?"

"That's the whole point!" Mr. Wakefield replied. "I've never done one single thing that wasn't for completely selfish reasons."

"I don't call working hard to support your family selfish," Mrs. Wakefield said. She looked stunned. "What could be more important?"

Jessica put her toast down and gaped at her parents. It seemed as though every single conversation between them ended up as an argument. And now they weren't even talking about Keith anymore, which was what *she* wanted to talk about!

"There's a lot more to life than just thinking about yourself," Mr. Wakefield said with a hard edge to his voice. "Here I am, in my forties, and *I've* never sat down in front of a weapons plant."

Mrs. Wakefield let out an incredulous laugh. "Then sit down in front of one, if that's the way you feel about it!"

"That's just an example," Mr. Wakefield said impatiently. "All I'm saying is, I've never made a difference in the world."

Jessica stood up suddenly. "Excuse me!" she said loudly. Her parents looked up at her in surprise. "Not that you care, but I'm going upstairs now." With a dramatic flourish, Jessica turned around and flounced out of the kitchen.

"My whole family is flipping out!" she grumbled, stomping up the stairs. Her parents were constantly bickering, and then there was Steven. One minute he was acting like a zombie and the next minute like the happiest person in the world. It was totally weird.

Jessica paused at the top of the stairs. Maybe Cara knew what was going on with Steven, she thought. Then she remembered yesterday afternoon. They had seen that girl who looked like Tricia Martin, and then Cara had suddenly started crying and run off.

Was her brother dating that girl? Could that be why he was acting so peculiar? And why had Cara shot out of the store like a nuclear missile?

"Hey, Liz?" Jessica called out, heading down the hall. She looked into her sister's room. Elizabeth glanced up from writing in her journal. "Do you know why Steve's acting so weird?" she asked.

Elizabeth looked down. "Well, I—"

"I think I know," Jessica went on knowingly. "There's this girl, see, who looks a *lot* like Tricia Martin—"

"I know," Elizabeth said quietly.

Jessica cocked one eyebrow. "Huh?"

"You're right." Elizabeth let out a heavy sigh. "It's pretty unbelievable."

"Hmm." Jessica folded her arms. "This is not

good news," she stated dryly. "What about Cara?"

Elizabeth shook her head. "I don't know."

"Well, I'm going to ask him!" Jessica said in a determined voice. "Where is he, anyway?"

"Hang gliding," Elizabeth told her.

Jessica gritted her teeth. "Well, when he gets home, I'm going to kill him."

Steven hoisted the glider harness onto his back and checked the buckles. His teacher, Bart, rechecked them.

"You're all set," Bart said, tapping Steven's helmet. "Are you ready? Are you with it?"

Nodding, Steven gripped the handlebar. He stared out straight over the edge of the cliff. "I'm with it."

"OK," Bart said. "Go for it. Just remember everything I've said, and you'll be fine."

Steven took a deep breath, lifted up, and ran to the edge. There was a sickening drop, and then he was soaring out above the canyon. The earth fell away under his feet as he rose up on the thermals like an eagle or a condor.

As the wind whistled around him and rippled the taut nylon wings, Steven forced himself to concentrate on what he was doing. But his thoughts kept drifting back to his fight with Cara. There were a hundred different ways that conversation could have gone. All of them would have been better than what actually had happened.

"How could I be such a jerk?" he said out loud. The rushing wind filled his mouth and forced Steven to pay attention. He swung his body to the left for a turn, and he came into line with the sun.

For a moment, the light dazzled his eyes. In his imagination, he saw Cara's face, and then Tricia's and Andrea's. He was sure he had loved Tricia, and he was pretty sure he was falling in love with Andrea, too.

But he still loved Cara, didn't he?

He shook his head to clear the images away, and his helmet slipped over one eye, blocking his vision. When he raised his hand to fix it, the glider lurched to the right, and then swooped down toward the cliff face.

Steven's pulse raced. He pulled out of the turn, but his helmet was still askew, and he couldn't see as well as he needed to. Was he supposed to pull up to go up, or up to go down? Suddenly, Steven realized he couldn't remember all the maneuvers correctly. The more he struggled to correct his position, the more wildly he swerved. He was losing altitude fast. The canyon floor was racing up to meet him.

"Come on! Come on!" Steven gasped, gritting his teeth. He dragged with all his strength on the handlebar, but one hand slipped off.

The glider dropped ten feet at once and then caught an air current and swooped up again. The harness gouged into his shoulders. Steven felt frantic—he couldn't control the glider at all! In horror, he watched the canyon trees come closer and closer. The ground sped by under his feet in a blinding rush. He was going to crash!

Steven closed his eyes and screamed.

Nine

"What am I going to do, Mom?" Cara asked, wiping a tear from her face.

Mrs. Walker gently brushed Cara's dark hair back. "Just take one day at a time, sweetheart. That's all you can do."

"I wish it were yesterday. I wish I could start all over."

"I know, *cara mia,* I know," her mother crooned, patting her back.

"Do you think he might call?" Cara went on hopefully. "He could, you know."

Mrs. Walker didn't say anything. Cara sniffed. She knew it was no use hoping.

But then the phone did ring!

"That could be him!" Cara gasped, jumping up off the couch. She ran to grab the telephone and almost dropped it. "Hello?"

"Cara?" came a tearful voice. "Cara? It's Jessica! Steven! He's—"

Cara froze. "What?" she whispered.

"He was in an accident! On the hang glider!" Jessica choked out. "They're taking him to the hospital. We're all going over right now!"

"But how bad is it?" Cara asked. "Will he—"

Jessica gulped for air. "They don't know! I think it's really bad! Are you coming?"

"Yes—no!" Cara clenched her fist. "I don't know—he doesn't want me, Jessica!"

"Cara, I have to go! You've got to come!" Jessica slammed the phone down.

Cara stood like a statue. She thought she was going to faint. She had to go to Steven and be with him. But he had made it clear just hours ago that they were finished. There was no place for her by his side now.

"Honey, what is it?" Mrs. Walker asked fearfully. "Sit down! You're as white as a sheet."

Cara turned blindly to her mother. "It's Steve," she said in a toneless voice. "He's been in an accident, and he's being taken to the hospital."

"Oh, how awful. Is he hurt badly?"

Tears started falling as Cara shook her head. "They don't know," she sobbed. She ran into her mother's arms and cried.

"I'll take you over to the hospital right now," her mother said.

Cara leaned back. "No! He doesn't want me," she insisted.

Her mother's eyes filled with tears, too. "Oh, honey." She sighed.

"He doesn't want me," Cara repeated in anguish.

Elizabeth gripped her twin's hand and stared at the doctor. She was explaining Steven's condition to the Wakefields. All around them, the controlled urgency of Fowler Memorial Hospital made a quiet, busy background.

"It's still too early to know for sure," Dr. Nichols said, folding her arms. "His left arm is broken, but we took care of that easily enough. And the contusions, cuts—we can deal with that. But it's the head injuries we can't be certain of. When we see the X rays, we'll have a better idea."

"When will he wake up?" Mrs. Wakefield asked in a hoarse voice.

Dr. Nichols shook her head and took off her glasses. "That's hard to say. He might be unconscious for just a short while, or it could be a matter of days."

Ned Wakefield went pale. Elizabeth saw him reach automatically for her mother's hand. "Can we see him?" he asked.

"Yes," the doctor said. "But I have to warn you, his face is quite bruised and swollen."

Elizabeth met her twin sister's eyes. Jessica looked frightened and vulnerable. Elizabeth squeezed her hand, and Jessica squeezed back. It was at times like this that Elizabeth needed her sister the most.

Without speaking, the Wakefields followed Dr. Nichols down the hallway. Elizabeth stared straight ahead at her mother's back. She had to be brave. Next to her, Jessica caught a shaky breath.

"He's in here," Dr. Nichols said, pushing open a swinging door.

The room was dark, but a shaded light shone down on the white bed. Elizabeth and her sister walked to their brother's side. Elizabeth bit back a gasp.

Steven's face was cut and bruised, and his left arm was in a cast. But worst of all was the gauze bandage that was wound around his head. It seemed ominous and threatening. His breathing was shallow and raspy.

"Omigod," Jessica breathed. Her chin was quivering, and she hugged herself tightly.

"Steven?" Mrs. Wakefield bent over him and put her cheek against his. "My little boy!" Her voice caught, and a tear dropped onto the pillow by Steven's head.

Mr. Wakefield put his arm across her shoulders and drew her to him. "He'll be OK," he said gruffly, hugging her and smoothing her hair. "He'll be all right."

Tactfully, Dr. Nichols picked up Steven's chart and stood near the door where it was lighter. She frowned as she read it over.

"Can we stay here?" Elizabeth asked Dr. Nichols. "With Steve?"

The doctor looked up and nodded in sympathy. "It might be a long wait," she warned gently.

"Dr. Nichols! Dr. Nichols to Emergency, stat!" said the intercom.

Elizabeth watched the doctor put back the chart.

"If you have any more questions, let me know," Dr. Nichols said in a brisk voice. She gave them an understanding smile. "I have to go."

Mr. and Mrs. Wakefield both nodded. The twins stood aside as the doctor hurried out. The room became very silent when the door shut.

"Do you think he'll wake up?" Jessica whispered, asking the question on everyone's mind.

"Of course he will, honey," Mrs. Wakefield said in a positive tone. She straightened her back, clearly trying to be strong for everyone. "We'll stay right here until he does. We'll help him get through this."

Elizabeth helped her sister pull the chairs that were in the room up to the bed. Mr. and Mrs. Wakefield remained standing by Steven's side, holding hands and looking down at their son.

After twenty minutes, Steven let out a muffled groan, but he didn't wake up. He moved his legs restlessly under the blanket and grimaced as though in pain.

"Steve?" Mrs. Wakefield whispered. "We're here, honey. We're right here."

He drew a deep breath in his uneasy sleep.

A half hour later, there was a soft tap on the door. Elizabeth turned around, expecting to see Dr. Nichols. Cara stood in the doorway, her face streaked with tears.

"I—how is he?" she whispered, staring at the bed. Her eyes were wide with sorrow and fear, but she didn't come any closer.

Jessica sniffled. "He's still unconscious."

Cara nodded.

"He's been saying a few words," Elizabeth added. "Just mumbling."

There was a rustle by the bed, and Elizabeth turned to see. Steven was moving his head from side to side on the pillow. Her parents hovered over him, watching anxiously. Mrs. Wakefield was holding his hand in both of hers.

"No—" Steven muttered, gritting his teeth and breathing hard. "I can't—"

Elizabeth squeezed her hands together.

"Should we call the doctor?" Jessica asked.

Nobody spoke.

"I can't—" Steven said fretfully. "Tricia!"

Elizabeth saw the color drain from Cara's face. With one hand over her mouth, Cara pushed her way through the door and ran down the corridor. For a moment, Elizabeth was tempted to go after her. But she couldn't leave her brother. Torn, she took a step toward the bed and then stopped.

"Cara?" Steven asked in a pitifully small voice. Then he sighed and was quiet.

Jessica gasped. "I'll tell her," she said, wide-eyed. She rushed out of the room.

"Steven?" Mrs. Wakefield said softly. She caressed his cheek. "We're here with you. Can you hear me?" But Steven was quiet.

The door opened, and Jessica walked listlessly back into the room. She met Elizabeth's eyes and shook her head.

"I couldn't find her," she whispered. "I think she must have gone home."

Mr. Wakefield stood up and gave the twins a tender smile. "Why don't you both go home, too?" he suggested. "We'll call if there's any change."

But Elizabeth shook her head, and Jessica said, "No way."

"We'll stay," Elizabeth added.

"It's going to be a long night," Alice Wakefield said in a faraway voice, looking down at Steven. Her husband put his arm around her.

Elizabeth nodded. As she looked at her parents, she realized in surprise that it was the first time in a long time she had seen them holding each other. It was wonderful to see them that way again, but Steven's accident was a terrible way to bring them together.

At that moment, Dr. Nichols opened the door. She was holding a number of large envelopes containing X rays. Everyone turned to her instantly.

"Why don't you all come out into the hall?" she suggested. "I'll show you the pictures."

Obediently, they trooped out after her. Dr. Nichols turned on a light by the nurses' station and held up the black films. Steven's skull was photographed from every angle.

"This is where he hit," the doctor said, pointing with a pen at one spot. "I don't see any fracture at all, not even a hairline fracture."

Elizabeth held her breath.

"Is that good?" Mrs. Wakefield interrupted, biting her lip.

"Well, yes, it's good," Dr. Nichols said gravely. "But Steven could still have sustained a serious concussion without a fracture. When the brain is shocked—jolted—like this, it can be badly bruised." She frowned. "It takes some time to heal itself."

"How much time?" Mr. Wakefield asked.

"That I can't say for sure," the doctor admitted. She tugged on the stethoscope around her neck. "We'll monitor Steven through the night and see how he is in the morning. If he doesn't wake up normally, we'll run some tests on him and see if we can figure out what's happening."

Elizabeth felt her stomach turn over. The scene felt unreal to her. It couldn't be *her* brother the doctor was discussing. It couldn't be *her* family that was huddled together, praying for Steven's recovery. More than anything else, Elizabeth wished she hadn't fought so much with her brother recently. Even though she had apologized to him just that morning, the bitter words between them still hurt.

"I don't want to go back in right away," Jessica whispered to her while their parents were talking in an undertone with the doctor.

Elizabeth nodded. Her throat was so tight she could hardly swallow. "Let's—let's go down to the cafeteria and get sodas or something."

Months earlier, both of them had worked as candy stripers at the hospital, so they knew their way around. But Elizabeth wished she had never been to the hospital and didn't have to be there right then.

The twins brought coffee for their parents when they returned to Steven's room. All through the night, they took turns sitting by

Steven's bed, pacing the halls, going to get food, or taking restless naps. It was a lonely vigil, even though they comforted each other as much as possible. Elizabeth had just heard the first sounds of breakfast being served to other patients when Steven let out a heavy sigh.

"Wha—" he said groggily.

Mrs. Wakefield, dozing in a chair, jerked awake instantly. Mr. Wakefield leaned over the bed. "Steve?" he whispered. "Steve, can you hear me?"

Elizabeth and Jessica stood at the foot of the bed. Steven grimaced, and his eyelids fluttered open. "Hey," Steven said in a thin voice. He managed a faint smile at his mother. "I bet I'm in big trouble, right?"

Mrs. Wakefield let out a laugh that was half a sob, too. "You sure are," she said, smiling through her tears.

"Oh, man," he groaned. "I'm so sore."

Elizabeth bit her lip to stop herself from crying. "Hi, Steve," she whispered. Jessica gave him a tiny wave and grinned.

Steven turned and tried to focus on the twins. "Hey, something's wrong—I'm seeing double."

They all laughed, then crowded around to kiss him. "We were so worried!" Jessica said, trying to hug him while avoiding the cast on his arm.

"I'll see if I can find the doctor," Mr. Wakefield said in a husky voice. He turned away quickly and wiped his eyes.

Elizabeth felt tears of relief fill her own eyes. It looked like Steven was going to pull through just fine.

Ten

Jessica picked Keith up at his house in Palisades on Monday night. She was borrowing her brother's car, since the Fiat was still in the shop. Steven didn't need the car while he was in the hospital, so she figured it was fair game.

"You drive a different car each time I see you," Keith said as he got in. "They aren't all yours, are they?"

Jessica laughed. "No, none of them are," she admitted, pulling into traffic. They were actually going to do something fun that night, for a change. They were going to see a movie and Jessica knew exactly what movie she wanted to see. She headed back toward Sweet Valley. "I know you don't believe in using fossil fuels, but *I'd* be a fossil if I had to walk everywhere."

"You don't look too decrepit," Keith said.

"Thanks." Jessica couldn't resist smiling at him. Finally, he was beginning to *notice!* It was about time they made a little progress.

"But, Jessica?" Keith said. His voice was low and intimate.

She felt her heart flutter. "Yes?"

Keith looked at her and then reached out one hand to touch her cheek. Jessica wished she didn't have to look at the road. She couldn't wait to hear what he was going to tell her. This time, she was positive he was going to say something romantic.

"You shouldn't stay in the sun too much," he said seriously. "With the ozone layer disappearing the way it is, ultraviolet light is getting stronger all the time. It's dangerous."

Jessica slumped in her seat and let her breath out slowly. "Thanks for the warning," she said, trying not to lose her patience. "I'll keep that in mind."

"It's just that skin cancer is a terrible disease to get," Keith went on. "I did this fund-raising thing for the Cancer Society last year—"

"Which movie should we go to?" Jessica interrupted. She was getting tired of hearing about all the wonderful, selfless things he did all the time. "There's that new thriller at the Valley Cinema about the detective who falls in love with the psycho killer. I heard it's supposed to be really hot."

"That?" Keith rested his elbow in the open window and scowled. "Commercial films are so mindless and predictable. It's just a waste of time, really. I thought we could see the documentary on the reindeer culture of the Lapps. It got really good reviews."

Jessica found it difficult to keep a straight face. "A documentary on reindeer?" she said. She threw him a skeptical smile as she drove. "I thought it would really be fun to see something exciting and romantic," she added.

"It's not just about the reindeer," Keith explained. "It's about the Laplanders and how their whole culture is self-contained and self-sufficient. It's really interesting."

Gritting her teeth, Jessica said, "But I just don't really feel like watching a documentary about Laplanders."

"Oh." Keith looked at her woodenly. "So you want to see that Hollywood garbage?"

Jessica shrugged. She was reaching a point

where she didn't care very much what Keith thought about her. So she wasn't as dedicated to world causes as he was. Big deal. "Yup," she said breezily.

He shrugged, too, and looked out the window. "OK. If that's what you want."

"That's what I want," she told him. "Sometimes you just have to go for mindless entertainment, Keith."

He looked very doubtful, but Jessica didn't worry about it.

By the time they got to the Valley Cinema, she was feeling very philosophical. Either it would work out with Keith or it wouldn't. But there was absolutely no way she was going to watch a documentary about reindeer. She parked the car, threw her bag over her shoulder, and set out with Keith across the parking lot.

"Hey—" she said suddenly, stopping in her tracks. Ahead of them was the girl from the Unique Boutique, the girl who looked like Tricia Martin. The girl Steven had dumped Cara for. Elizabeth had said her name was Andrea.

"What is it?" Keith asked.

Narrowing her eyes, Jessica watched as Andrea walked up to a tall boy with dark hair who was waiting at the cinema entrance. He smiled and put his arm across her shoulders. They walked inside together.

"What's wrong?" Keith asked again.

Jessica snapped her attention back to him. "Oh, sorry," she said. "I just saw something very interesting."

Steven looked up from his magazine as the door opened. Dr. Nichols came in, giving him a friendly smile. After two days in the hospital, Steven felt as though they were old friends. He returned her smile quickly.

"Hi, Dr. Nichols," Steven said. He hitched himself up awkwardly in the bed. He usually felt a little bit embarrassed to be seen in his hospital gown, but Dr. Nichols never made him feel self-conscious.

"How's it going, Steve?" she asked. She glanced at his chart and clicked her pen several times. Then she looked at him over the rims of her glasses. "Does your head still hurt?"

Steven touched the bandage gingerly and gave her an exaggerated wince. "Yeah, but it's not too bad. They gave me some of those capsules at lunchtime."

"Good." She leaned forward and touched his

forehead with long, slender fingers. "I think you're doing just fine," she announced. "How's the arm? Gets in your way, right?"

"Right," Steven laughed, glancing at his cast. "But it's OK. It aches a bit, that's all." Even if it had hurt more, Steven wouldn't have admitted it. The sooner he got out of the hospital, the better. He was still full of aches and pains, and limping across the room was torture. But he wanted to go home.

Dr. Nichols made a note on his chart and then smiled. "Feel like going home soon?"

"You bet!" Steven gasped, amazed. "You read my mind! Can I go today?"

"Whoa!" Dr. Nichols laughed and shook her head. "Not today. Let's say the day after tomorrow. You're not completely out of the woods yet, but I think you can rest at home just as well as you can here. And I mean *rest*," she added firmly.

"I will," Steven said, nodding. His head began to throb, and he quickly held it still. "I will," he repeated contritely.

Dr. Nichols grinned in sympathetic understanding. "See what I mean? You banged yourself up pretty badly, so take it easy. Tell your parents to ask for me this evening when they come to visit you. I'll fill them in."

"Great," Steven said. He watched her go out and then lay back with a sigh of relief. Knowing he was going to be discharged in two days made him feel much better.

For the first time, he wished there was someone in the other bed. There was nobody to share his news with. He snapped his fingers absently. Then he picked up the telephone. He wanted to talk to Andrea and tell her. She had stopped over the day before for a very brief visit after he had called her. Brimming with eagerness, he punched in the shop phone number.

"Unique Boutique. Can I help you?" The voice was that of an older woman.

Steven eased his broken arm carefully. "Yes, can I speak to Andrea, please?"

"I'm sorry, she's helping a customer right now. Can I give her a message?"

Steven frowned. She would be coming over soon anyway. He guessed he could wait until then.

"No, that's all right," he said. "I'll talk to her later."

When he hung up the phone, Steven lay back and stared moodily at the white ceiling. It seemed ironic to him that it took a serious accident to put everything into perspective. Even though he had started hang gliding to get Andrea out of his mind, he had come to realize that it was a foolish mistake. He couldn't get her out of his mind, and he didn't want to, either.

Trying to curb his impatience, Steven picked up his magazine again and flipped through it, but he tossed it aside the moment he heard a tap on the open door. His sisters were standing in the doorway.

"Hey," he called. "Welcome to my private suite."

Jessica held up two fingers. "How many?" she teased.

Steven looked innocent. "Two. But there's one thing I'm not sure about—who are you?"

"Har-de-har-har." Jessica smirked at him.

"How do you feel, Steve?" Elizabeth asked.

Jessica perched on the empty bed. "You still look awful."

Steven laughed. "Thanks. I feel—uh . . ." He frowned thoughtfully and tried not to smile. "How can I describe it? Crummy? No, that's not exactly right. Lousy? No. Unbelievably—"

"Cut it out," Jessica broke in with a giggle. "You sure aren't behaving like you're sick. Is this all just an act?"

"Why are you in such a good mood?" Elizabeth asked, pulling up a chair.

"Dr. Nichols was just here," Steven explained. He struggled to sit up a bit, and Elizabeth adjusted the pillows for him. "Thanks. She says I can go home day after tomorrow."

Elizabeth and Jessica shared a happy look. "That's great," Jessica crowed. "But I know you can't drive yet, so I'm still borrowing your car."

"Jess!" Elizabeth said in a shocked voice. She tossed an empty paper cup at her sister's head and Jessica ducked.

Steven grinned. "I don't mind," he said. He rested his head against the pillows and looked at the ceiling unconcernedly.

"OK, Steve," Elizabeth said in a laughing voice. "We give up. Why *else* are you in such a good mood?"

He just smiled.

"He's trying to act mysterious," Jessica said to Elizabeth. "Ignore him." Then to Steven she added, "Let me sign your cast. I want to be the first one."

"Be my guest," Steven said lightly. As she dug around in her purse for a pen, he added, "And then you two have to beat it. I'm expecting someone. A VIV—Very Important Visitor."

"Well, ex-c-u-u-se me." Jessica giggled. She began scribbling something on his arm.

"Andrea?" Elizabeth asked in a distant tone.

The look on her face irritated Steven. "I wish you wouldn't act that way, Liz."

"What way?" she replied.

Jessica was drawing a big, loopy flower. "Who's Andrea? Oh—that girl who looks like Tricia?" she asked, glancing at her twin. "I saw her last night at the movies," she went on. "With some guy."

No one spoke. Jessica was still scrawling on Steven's cast. Steven could hear his heart beating.

"What guy?" he asked finally, trying to keep his voice natural.

Jessica shrugged. "I don't know who he was, but they looked pretty friendly."

"Jessica—" Elizabeth warned.

"What do you mean?" Steven pressed. Part of him wanted Jessica to go on, and part of him wanted her to shut up. But he had to know.

Jessica recapped her pen and hopped onto the other bed again. She dangled her legs over the side. She seemed to have no idea of the effect she was having on Steven. "Well, for starters," she chattered, "he had his arm around her."

Steven felt his face heat up. He tried to laugh casually. "Oh, he's probably just her brother or a good friend."

Instead of answering, Jessica raised her eyebrows. Her face was a picture of skepticism.

Angrily, Steven pushed the covers aside and swung his legs over the side of the bed. He couldn't stand lying still.

"Here," Elizabeth offered, coming to his side and taking his arm.

"Thanks," he said gruffly.

With Elizabeth's help, he limped to the window and stood looking out. From there, he had a view of the main entrance to the hospital. Cars and taxis pulled up to the front, letting people out or picking them up. Steven watched a new mother, her baby in her arms, come out in a wheelchair and wait on the curb.

"Steve?" Elizabeth said softly.

He didn't answer. He just kept watching the entrance to the hospital. He didn't want to think about what Jessica had said and what she was implying. It couldn't be true, and besides, it was making his head start throbbing again. He drew a deep breath and rubbed his temples.

"Steve, what about Cara?" Elizabeth insisted.

"Liz, can't you see I'm—" Steven broke off, staring at the driveway below.

Elizabeth moved the curtain aside for a better look. Steven knew she could see what he was seeing. A convertible with a young, dark-haired man at the wheel had stopped by the curb. Andrea was in the passenger seat. There was no mistaking her curly, strawberry-blond hair.

His heart pounding, Steven stared down at them. He wanted to believe there was nothing to worry about. He wanted to believe that the guy was Andrea's brother or cousin. But the next moment, Andrea leaned toward the driver and kissed him. It was not a sisterly kiss. Steven's stomach lurched.

"Steve, I'm sor—" Elizabeth began.

"It's nothing," Steven interrupted, turning away. He walked stiffly back to the bed and sank down onto it. His eyes were filled with tears.

Jessica was looking around in wide-eyed confusion. "What? What is it?"

"Let's go, Jess," Elizabeth said.

"What? Why?" Frowning, Jessica stood up. "We just got here two seconds ago."

"Let's go," Elizabeth repeated firmly.

Dragging Jessica with her, Elizabeth left the room and shut the door behind them. Out in the hallway, Jessica refused to go a step further.

"What is the big idea, Liz?" she asked indignantly. "Why are you and Steven suddenly acting so bizarre?"

Elizabeth puffed out her cheeks and let the air out slowly. "You know why, Jessica. You did that on purpose, didn't you?"

Jessica's eyes had a guarded look. She shrugged and dug her hands into her pockets. "What do you mean?"

"You deliberately blabbed all that stuff about Andrea," Elizabeth accused her. "You know Steve was going out with her."

Jessica licked her lips. "Well . . ." She looked up at the ceiling for a few moments. "Cara's one of my best friends," she said at last. "I just thought Steven should know his perfect Andrea isn't so perfect, that's all."

Elizabeth nodded silently. She was partly furious with Jessica for hurting Steven on purpose. But she was partly glad, too. Maybe it was just what their brother needed to snap out of his fixation on that girl. And besides, if Andrea was seeing another boy, Steven ought to know that.

Of course, there were subtler ways to break bad news. It wasn't necessary to hit him over the head with a sledgehammer, but that was

Jessica's way. She always used a sledgehammer when a gentle tap would do the job. "But it was pretty rough on Steve to see her kissing that guy."

"Kissing what guy?" Jessica asked. "Is that what you saw out the window? Liz, I didn't plan *that*! I had no idea she'd suddenly appear."

Elizabeth sighed. "You couldn't have known," she agreed. "I guess . . . ." Elizabeth began. She shook her head and gave her twin a rueful smile. "I guess you did the right thing."

Jessica held up her hands. "I always do the right thing, Liz."

"Yeah, sure," Elizabeth said wryly. She frowned, deep in thought. "You know what we should do?"

Their eyes met. Jessica nodded. At the same time they both said, "Call Cara."

"Come on," Elizabeth said. They hurried down the corridor toward the pay phone.

Elizabeth felt guilty about Cara. With all the anxiety about Steven, she hadn't had time to give a thought to Cara. But now that Elizabeth stopped to consider, she knew Cara must have been going through a pretty rough time on her own.

"Give me a quarter," Jessica said, holding out her hand.

Elizabeth snapped open her wallet. "Here."

While Jessica dialed Cara's number, Elizabeth paced nervously back and forth. What they were doing definitely qualified as meddling. But Elizabeth was positive Steven had been going off on a wild goose chase with Andrea. Whatever had gone wrong between him and Cara never should have happened. So if there was a chance to make it right again, Elizabeth thought they should take it.

"Just don't tell her Andrea's going to be here, whatever you do," Elizabeth whispered.

Jessica nodded and put one hand on Elizabeth's shoulder. "Just leave it to me, Liz. I know what to do."

"I sure hope so," Elizabeth muttered. All she could do was pray they were doing the right thing by calling.

Then it would be up to Cara.

Eleven

Steven groaned with frustration as he tried to struggle into a pair of jeans. He knew he couldn't face Andrea in a hospital gown; he felt vulnerable enough already. His broken arm was heavy and awkward in its cast, and he was breathing hard in pain and exasperation, but he managed to pull himself together just in time. There was a hesitant knock on the door.

"Come in," he croaked, standing with his back against the window. He knew he couldn't hide the anger and hurt that he was feeling.

Andrea pushed the door open and came in smiling. But her smile faded when she saw the expression on Steven's face.

"Who is he?" Steven said, staring at her accusingly. He wanted to be calm, but his voice almost cracked. He hoped she would say it was all just a simple misunderstanding.

Andrea let her breath out slowly. "He's a friend, Steve," she said. "I met him last week, and I really like him a lot."

"But—" Steven paused. "How can you do this to me? After all we've been through?"

"After all we've been through?" Andrea repeated in a wondering voice. She shook her head sadly. "Steve, we've been out maybe five times altogether. Don't get me wrong, I've enjoyed it. You're a really nice person. But we never made any promises to each other!"

Steven gaped at her. "Never made any promises! How can you say that? You know how I feel about you!"

"I know how you feel about *Tricia*," Andrea said. She held his gaze. "All the time we've been together, you've been projecting your memory of Tricia onto me."

"That's not true," Steven said defensively. He sank down on the chair by the window and tried to collect his thoughts. He felt weak and tired.

"Yes, it is." Andrea paced nervously back

and forth across the small hospital room. She held out one hand in an imploring gesture, and her face looked very sad. "Steve, you've never really seen me or heard me or gotten to know *me, Andrea.* You want me to replace Tricia for you, and I can't do that."

"I do see you," Steven said. But his voice lacked real conviction. He didn't know what to think.

"Steve." Andrea sat down on the edge of the bed across from him and looked seriously into his eyes. "I'm really, really sorry about Tricia. I know you must have loved her a lot, and I realize you still miss her. But I found someone who likes me for who I am, not for who I remind him of."

"But . . ." Steven was slowly shaking his head and staring at the floor. He couldn't believe what he was hearing. But he had to admit that Andrea's words rang true. "I didn't mean to. . . ."

Andrea shrugged. She had sympathetic tears in her eyes. "I know you didn't mean to. But I still don't think this is going to work out between us. I'd never know if it was really me you liked."

Steven raised his head to look at her, and for

the first time, he really saw Andrea. He saw a girl who resembled Tricia in many ways, but who had her own ideas and her own feelings. He realized he had been leading her into situations that reproduced his times with Tricia. He had encouraged her to order food Tricia liked and talk about things Tricia had been interested in. He had wanted her to wear her hair the way Tricia did. He had taken her to places he and Tricia used to go to. In all that time, he had never really known—or tried to find out—how Andrea felt. He had just made her conform to his memories of Tricia.

"I'm sorry," he whispered, his eyes wide. "I'm really sorry."

"It's OK," Andrea replied with a wistful smile. "I understand. I just hope you do."

Steven nodded, and they were silent for a minute, each of them deep in thought. Then Steven cleared his throat.

"I guess this is where we say we can still be friends, right?" he said. He tried to make it sound lighthearted, but his voice was thick with emotion.

Andrea shook her head. "I don't think that would work out, Steve," she said gently. She stood up slowly. "I hope you get well soon."

Nodding, Steven looked away. He didn't want her to see the tears in his eyes. "Thanks," he said. He kept his face turned away while Andrea went to the door.

She stood there for a silent moment. Steven knew she was looking at him, but he couldn't trust himself to speak. Then she left.

For several minutes, Steven felt paralyzed. He couldn't think, couldn't feel. He was numb.

The full impact of what had happened gradually soaked in. He knew he would never see Tricia again—and that he could never replace her with another girl. He gave himself over to deep, wrenching grief. He buried his face in his hands and cried.

When his tears finally stopped, Steven stood and gazed forlornly out the window. He felt as if he had lost everything. And he realized that the worst loss of all was Cara. When he remembered the way he had treated her, he felt miserable.

"I'll never get her back," he whispered, resting his forehead against the cool windowpane. "She'll never come back to me. I've been such a jerk."

He knew Cara deserved someone better than he. No matter how lonely and sad he was, he could never ask her to forgive him. He couldn't leave her for another girl and then go begging her to come back now that the other girl was gone. It wasn't fair.

Cara's hands trembled on the steering wheel as she drove to the hospital. She knew she would never forget hearing Steven call out to Tricia. But Jessica had pleaded with Cara to come see him. Jessica wouldn't say why.

It didn't really matter. Even if Steven wanted her, Cara wouldn't go back to him now. She had been through enough pain and disappointment. She would see him this once, for Jessica. Then it was time to get on with life without Steven Wakefield.

Cara made herself walk slowly when she crossed the parking lot to the side entrance of the hospital. Inside, there was a quiet, cool air of efficiency. She passed the reception desk and headed for the elevator. She kept her chin up, and by the time she reached Steven's floor she had a polite but detached smile on her face. She wasn't going to risk getting hurt. She had to save her pride, at least. All the way down the hall, she concentrated on putting one foot in front of the other.

The door to Steven's room was open. She paused on the threshold, wondering frantically what to say. But then she saw that he was sitting by the window, looking out, and hadn't noticed her yet. The lamp over the bed threw a pool of light across the middle of the room, but Steven was in semi-shadow. She waited for a moment, just watching him in the silent twilight.

The way Steven was sitting made him look so lonesome and vulnerable that Cara felt her heart melt. She had never seen him look so sad. Instinct told her that he wanted to be alone, that he would be angry with her for intruding. She turned to go.

"Cara?"

Cheeks burning, Cara turned, keeping her gaze on the floor. "I just wanted to see if you were getting better," she said quietly.

Steven didn't speak, and Cara felt tears well up. Her resolve to be cool disappeared. "Steve—I just wanted to tell you something," she rushed on, hating herself for becoming so emotional. She raised her eyes briefly, but she still couldn't make out his expression. He was sitting as still as a statue. "I know you'll always love Tricia, and I know I never meant as much to you as she did," she said. "But I want you to know, our relationship was wonderful while it lasted and I'll always remember you. You'll always be special to me." Her voice died away to a whisper.

She stood where she was for a moment. He still didn't say anything, and Cara was sure she had made a fool of herself. Mortified, she turned back to the door.

"Cara, wait," Steven choked out.

She looked over her shoulder. Steven was pulling himself up out of the chair, and he moved into the circle of light. What Cara saw made her heart stop, and then start racing. He had tears in his eyes.

"Cara—can you—" He broke off and turned away.

"Can I what?" she asked.

"No, forget it."

When he shook his head, Cara clenched her fists. No! She wouldn't let herself hope. But she had to know what Steven was thinking. "Can I what?" she repeated in a firmer voice.

"No, I can't ask you," he said heavily.

Cara strode across the room and planted herself in front of him. "What can't you ask me?" she demanded, forcing him to meet her gaze.

Steven looked searchingly into her eyes. "Did you mean it? What you just said?"

For a moment, Cara thought she would cry. "Of course I did! I meant every word of it," she told him. She took a deep breath. She felt as if she were about to jump off the high dive without knowing if there was water below. "I still love you, Steven," she whispered.

They didn't speak. They stared at each other for a long moment. Then Steven reached out his good arm and touched her shoulder. With a sigh of relief, Cara stepped closer and hugged him tight.

"I love you too—ow, my arm." Steven winced, moving his cast.

Cara let out a laugh that was part sob. "Sorry," she sniffled, resting her cheek against his chest.

He hugged her awkwardly with one arm. "I'm the one who's sorry," he murmured into her hair. "I acted like such a jerk. I'm so sorry, Cara."

"It's OK," Cara said quickly, tightening her arms around him. "Is it over? You aren't seeing her anymore?"

Instead of answering, Steven pulled back and

looked into her eyes again. He kissed her tenderly. And then Cara knew it would be all right. She pressed her face into his neck and started to cry.

Jessica stopped pacing and faced her sister. "Come *on*, Liz. Let's see if she came."

Elizabeth didn't look up from her magazine. They were waiting in the hospital lounge. "You know Cara came. We saw her. She's been here for twenty minutes."

"Liz, just come on," Jessica begged. She grabbed her twin sister's hand and started tugging.

"Cut it out! You can be such a pest!" Elizabeth laughed. "All right. We'll go up to Steve's room," she said. "But if Cara is still there, we leave, right?"

"Right, right," Jessica said. She couldn't wait to see if their re-matchmaking scheme had worked. "What if they just got in a huge fight?" she mused.

Elizabeth sent her an irritated look and punched the elevator button. "Don't be so pessimistic."

"What if Steven's decided to swear off women

for the rest of his life?" Jessica went on. She was beginning to wonder if they had made a huge mistake. "What if Cara hates me for the rest of *my* life?"

When Elizabeth didn't answer, Jessica folded her arms and scowled at her feet. The elevator slid to a stop, the doors opened, and Elizabeth led the way. Jessica hurried behind her. As they approached Steven's room, however, Elizabeth slowed down and held up her hand. They tiptoed the rest of the way.

Holding her breath, Jessica peeked in. She was hoping for the best and expecting the worst. But when she saw her brother and Cara locked in a tight embrace, she let out a sigh of relief.

"Shh," Elizabeth said, jumping back and pulling Jessica with her.

"I guess we did it, huh?" Jessica whispered.

Elizabeth nodded. "I guess we did." Then her eyes widened as she looked past Jessica's shoulder. "Here come Mom and Dad!"

"Yikes! Let's stop them," Jessica hissed.

They hurried down the hall to head off their parents.

"Hi, girls," Mrs. Wakefield called out. "How's Steve?"

Elizabeth walked up to her father, took his

arm, and turned him around. Jessica did the same to their mother.

"What the—" Mr. Wakefield said as he was steered back down the corridor.

"Girls, what are you doing?" Mrs. Wakefield asked.

"He's fine," Jessica announced in a soothing voice. "He just needs a little privacy right now."

Their parents looked completely baffled. Jessica glanced at Elizabeth and winked. Everything was going to be just fine!

Twelve

Two days later, Jessica and Cara headed out to the athletic fields for cheerleading practice. Jessica swung her pink duffel bag back and forth, chatting about Keith. Cara looked like she was in a dream. She and Steven were back together and more in love than before. But Jessica didn't want to talk about *them*.

"So then he looks right into my eyes," Jessica said with an exaggerated shiver. "And he asks me, 'Would you ever go on a fast?' I thought I would die. He's so ridiculous."

Cara giggled. "What did you tell him? Did you say you'd starve yourself for him?"

"Not exactly," Jessica replied. There was a

mischievous gleam in her eyes. "I thought about saying something like, 'If you'd just kiss me I wouldn't need to eat—"

"Stop!" Cara shrieked, giving Jessica a playful slap on the wrist. "You are so bad."

"I know. But I'm fed up with him, really. I don't think he's worth it."

"So . . . ?" Cara's voice trailed off.

"Soooo . . ." Jessica shrugged and reached a decision. She wanted a boy who paid more attention to her than to aluminum cans. "I guess I'm dumping him."

Cara sighed. "Poor Keith."

Jessica laughed and tossed her bag onto the grass as they reached the other cheerleaders. Everyone else was huddled together in a bunch. Jessica and Cara strolled over to join the laughing group.

"What's going on?" Jessica asked.

The huddle broke apart. Robin Wilson, the other co-captain, nodded at Maria Santelli. "Tell them, Maria," she said, smiling.

"It's so exciting," Sandy Bacon added.

Jessica arched her eyebrows. "What?"

"It's my father," Maria said. Her dark brown eyes were sparkling with excitement. "He just made it official. He's running for mayor."

"Isn't that cool?" broke in Jean West. She began clapping her hands in a syncopated rhythm. "S-A-N-T-E—" she chanted. The others laughed.

"Do you get to work on his campaign?" Cara asked. "Do you think he'll make any TV ads?"

Jean and Sandy both gasped. "Wouldn't it be great to make an ad *here*?" Sandy said excitedly. "I mean, it would make sense, right, Maria? You could be in it, and so could all your friends!"

"Right! Sweet Valley High on TV," Robin said, grinning. She looked at Maria. "If we could vote, we'd vote for your dad—but only if he put us on the tube."

"I don't know," Maria laughed, shaking her head. "I think that kind of campaign advertising is pretty expensive. He'll probably just do posters and make speeches and things. And maybe something on the radio."

Jessica began stretching out her legs. "Get him to go for the TV ads, Maria," she counseled. "That's what really gets the votes."

"She's a real expert," Cara told the others, pointing to Jessica behind her hand and grinning.

Jessica stuck her tongue out at her friend. "I just happen to know it's true, that's all," she said, trying not to smile. "Now let's get started, OK?"

Everyone quickly warmed up, and they ran through their cheers. Robin had created a new one, and they spent most of the afternoon perfecting it. Part of the new routine included a pyramid, but they were all feeling too giddy to do it without toppling over every time. As they were packing up to go, Jessica heard a familiar car horn. She looked over at the parking lot and let out a yell.

"Liz! Our car!" She broke into a run.

Elizabeth was sitting up on the back of the seat, waving and smiling. Their red Fiat convertible looked as good as new. Ecstatic, Jessica threw her duffel into the tiny back seat.

"It works? No more weird noises and stalling out at every single stop sign?" she asked breathlessly as Cara walked up.

"It works perfectly," Elizabeth said. She waved at the passenger seat. "May I offer you a lift, madame?"

Jessica bowed. "Thank you, madame."

"Cara," Elizabeth went on, "Mom just went to pick up Steve at the hospital, and we're having a welcome-home dinner. We want you to come."

Jessica's eyes lit up, and she grabbed her friend's hand. "Yes! You have to come, Cara. Steve would have a relapse if you didn't."

"Count me in," Cara agreed. She poked Jessica in the ribs. "I get to sit on your lap."

Jessica groaned and opened the door. "And you weigh a ton, Walker."

Laughing, Elizabeth slid down into her seat and started the engine. They were all in a good mood, and they laughed and sang along with the radio all the way home. A few minutes later, they pulled into the Wakefield driveway. Both of their parents' cars were already there.

"They're back!" Jessica said. She jounced Cara on her knees. "Get up, you load!"

"Jessica!" Cara laughed and tumbled out. The three girls trooped into the house.

"We're out on the patio!" Mrs. Wakefield called.

Steven was sitting in a lounge chair, sipping some iced tea. His eyes lit up when he saw Cara. Jessica and Elizabeth shared a knowing look. Prince Albert came over, tail wagging, to have his ears scratched.

"Hey, Steve," Jessica said as she flopped into a chair.

"Hi," he replied. His gaze was on Cara.

"It's great you could come, Cara," Mr. Wakefield said, giving her a warm smile.

"Thanks for inviting me," she said politely. She didn't take her eyes off Steven, though.

Elizabeth sat down next to her father. "How come you got home early, Dad?"

He gave her a wry smile. "I'm not a complete slave to my law practice," he told her.

"Boy, you could have fooled me," Jessica retorted. She reached for the iced tea pitcher and noticed an irritated frown on her mother's face.

"That's not funny, Jessica," Mrs. Wakefield said.

Jessica shrugged. "*Sorrr*-eee." As far as she could tell, her father *was* a slave to his law practice. And it didn't seem to give him very much satisfaction, either. At least, not judging by his general level of crabbiness over the past few weeks.

"When do we get to eat?" Steven asked. "After that awful hospital food, I feel like having tacos or barbecued chicken or something."

Mrs. Wakefield looked surprised. "But, Steve, your doctor prescribed a diet of boiled fish, rice pudding, and lima beans."

Jessica grabbed her throat and let out a groan of agony. "A fate worse than death," she gasped. Elizabeth and Cara both pretended to be swooning. Prince Albert barked and nudged Elizabeth's knee with his nose.

"No, come on, Mom," Steve said. "Dr. Nichols didn't really say anything like that, did she?"

"Awww," Elizabeth teased.

Mrs. Wakefield shrugged. "Doctor's orders," she went on in an apologetic voice.

"Right," Cara went on. She shook her head sadly. "If you want to get your strength back, you have to eat lots of nutritious foods like tofu—"

"Steamed cabbage," Jessica interrupted.

"Cod liver oil," Elizabeth added, looking solemnly at her brother.

"You guys!" Steven yelled.

"Now, give him a break." Mr. Wakefield laughed. "Whatever you want, Steve. You just name it and it's yours."

Mrs. Wakefield tipped her head to one side. "Whatever you want, as long as it's steak. That's what I got."

"You could always go out for something else," Mr. Wakefield pointed out. "After all, it *is* his first night home. He should have something special."

"Thanks for volunteering my time to go shopping," Mrs. Wakefield said with a somewhat indignant laugh. There was a hard edge to her words, however. "I'll be happy to prepare the *steak* any way Steven wants it."

Jessica sent a worried glance at her sister. A

moment ago, everyone had been joking and laughing and having a good time. Suddenly there was tension in the air. Every little thing got on their parents' nerves lately. The slightest issue turned into a problem, and the most minor problem turned into an argument. Elizabeth's jaw muscles tightened as she gritted her teeth. Cara looked embarrassed.

"Steak would be fine, Mom," Steven put in quickly. He was looking nervously at his parents.

Mrs. Wakefield smiled. "Should I grill it or cut it up and stir-fry it?" she asked. "You decide."

Jessica could tell by the expression on Steven's face that he was feeling uncomfortable. Jessica knew the feeling. Somehow, there was a sense that no matter what Steven said, it would make their father angry with their mother, or the other way around.

"If it's not too much trouble, grilling it would be fine," he mumbled.

There was an uneasy silence. Jessica rattled the ice cubes in her glass. "Hey, you know what?" she said brightly, trying to ease the tension. Everyone looked at her expectantly. "Maria Santelli's father is running for mayor."

"Peter Santelli?" Mr. Wakefield said. "I'm

surprised he didn't tell me. We've known each other for years. He's done a good job as city planning commissioner, and I think he'd make a good mayor."

"Maybe I can interview him and Maria for the school paper," Elizabeth put in. "You know, how does it feel to have a father in politics, that sort of thing."

"Something you'll never know firsthand, thank goodness," Mrs. Wakefield said.

"I don't know why you say that," her husband retorted. "I'd hate to think I'll never do anything for this community. It's not as though being a lawyer till the end of my days excites me."

Mrs. Wakefield threw her hands up in a gesture of exasperation. "Then stop *being* a lawyer if it makes you so unhappy, Ned!" she burst out. "Don't take it out on us!"

"Oh, right," he replied, standing up. "Just like that? Quit my job? Good thinking, Alice— Steve's in college, and the girls will be there soon." He dug his hands into his pockets, scowled at the swimming pool, and then turned and walked into the house.

Mrs. Wakefield sank into her chair and glowered at his retreating figure. She began absently twisting her wedding ring around and around her finger, and she looked agitated.

Jessica glanced apprehensively at the others. Elizabeth was busy scratching the dog's chest and pretending to be oblivious to the situation. Steven and Cara began talking about renting a movie to watch on the VCR.

Jessica felt hurt and confused and alone. "Mom?" she said, turning to her mother.

Mrs. Wakefield stood up and sent Jessica a preoccupied smile. "Excuse me, honey, I'll be right back." She strode toward the house after Mr. Wakefield.

Jessica felt a lump in her throat. What was going on? What was happening to her parents?

Is there serious trouble brewing between Mr. and Mrs. Wakefield? Find out in Sweet Valley High #65, **TROUBLE AT HOME.**

Series
Don't miss any of the Caitlin trilogies
Created by Francine Pascal

There has never been a heroine quite like the raven-haired, unforgettable beauty, Caitlin. Dazzling, charming, rich, and very, very clever Caitlin Ryan seems to have everything. Everything, that is, but the promise of lasting love. The three trilogies follow Caitlin from her family life at Ryan Acres, to Highgate Academy, the exclusive boarding school in the posh horse country of Virginia, through college, and on to a glamorous career in journalism in New York City.

Don't miss Caitlin!

Celebrate the Seasons
with SWEET VALLEY HIGH
Super Editions

You've been a SWEET VALLEY HIGH fan all along—
hanging out with Jessica and Elizabeth and their friends
at Sweet Valley High. And now the SWEET VALLEY
HIGH *Super Editions* give you more of what you like
best—more romance—more excitement—more real-life
adventure! Whether you're bicycling up the California
Coast in PERFECT SUMMER, dancing at the Sweet
Valley Christmas Ball in SPECIAL CHRISTMAS, touring
the South of France in SPRING BREAK, catching the
rays in a MALIBU SUMMER, or skiing the snowy slopes
in WINTER CARNIVAL—you know you're exactly
where you want to be—with the gang from SWEET
VALLEY HIGH.

SWEET VALLEY HIGH SUPER EDITIONS

☐ **PERFECT SUMMER** ☐ **MALIBU SUMMER**
  25072/$2.95   26050/$2.95

☐ **SPRING BREAK**   ☐ **WINTER CARNIVAL**
  25537/$2.95   26159/$2.95

☐ **SPECIAL CHRISTMAS** ☐ **SPRING FEVER**
  25377/$2.95   26420/$2.95

- -

Bantam Books, Dept. SVS2, 414 East Golf Road, Des Plaines, IL 60016

Please send me the items I have checked above. I am enclosing $_____
(please add $2.00 to cover postage and handling). Send check or money
order, no cash or C.O.D.s please.

Mr/Ms _____

Address _____

City/State _____ Zip _____

Please allow four to six weeks for delivery.   SVS2—11/89
Prices and availability subject to change without notice.

YOUR OWN

SLAM BOOK!

If you've read *Slambook Fever*, Sweet Valley High #48, you know that slam books are the rage at Sweet Valley High. Now *you* can have a slam book of your own! Make up your own categories, such as "Biggest Jock" or "Best Looking," and have your friends fill in the rest! There's a four-page calendar, horoscopes and questions most asked by Sweet Valley readers with answers from Elizabeth and Jessica.

It's a must for SWEET VALLEY fans!

☐ 05496 FRANCINE PASCAL'S SWEET
VALLEY HIGH SLAM BOOK
Laurie Pascal Wenk $3.95